MW00936408

Heaven Between Her Thighs 2: Stealing His Heart

A Novel By

Denora Boone

Text ROYALTY to

42828 to join our

mailing list!

To submit a manuscript for our review,

email us at

submissions@royaltypublishinghouse.co

m

Text RPHCHRISTIAN to 22828 for our

CHRISTIAN ROMANCE novels!

Text RPHROMANCE to 22828 for our

INTERRACIAL ROMANCE novels!

Heaven Between Her Thighs
Denora Boone

© 2016

Published by Royalty Publishing House

www.royaltypublishinghouse.com

-1-

The room was pitch black thanks to the blackout curtains that covered the large windows in the bedroom. It had to be about 50 degrees in the large space but the thick orange and black comforter blocked out just enough of the frigid air while letting in the right amount for her to remain comfortable. The only sound that could be heard was the powerful voice of KeKe Wyatt floating through the surround sound speakers above her head. Anything louder than that would have caused the migraine that she had just gotten rid of to come back, and if she planned on getting anything done that day, she needed it to stay at bay.

Before she could muster up any energy to get up, the door to her inner sanctum was pushed open and a silhouette appeared. She already knew who it was without even seeing the person's features clearly. Not speaking a word, they walked over to the window and opened the curtains, followed by the blinds. The light was so bright she had to close her eyes and tuck her head further down underneath her blanket.

"Oh no, ma'am. We are not doing this another doggone day. Now I let you slide the first few days after everything happened, but today it's time to get up," Von said, standing over Chey while she tried to hide.

"Not today, Von," Chey said, sinking deeper into the king sized mattress. She figured if she whined a little Von would let her be, but that was just wishful thinking on her part.

Ignoring Chey, Von snatched the covers back and placed her hands on her hips. The look on her face was telling Chey that she better not try her and her best bet would be to get on up. As bad as she didn't want to, she knew she'd better or risk dealing with a lashing from Von.

Sitting up on the side of the bed, she had to get her bearings together. The room seemed to be spinning and the last thing she wanted to do was throw up again. That migraine had her doing enough of that for the last few days.

"I got your clothes out for today and breakfast will be ready by the time you get downstairs," Von informed her before walking out of the room. There was no use in arguing,

2

so Chey got on up and took care of her body, face, and hair before getting dressed.

Looking in the mirror, she may have looked better on the outside but her insides were still all over the place. For the life of her, she couldn't get the revelation out of her mind that Qyree's mother, Zaria, had laid on them all a few months prior.

"Natalia, you and the help here," Zaria started as she tilted her head towards Toni, "may want to go get tested before you have that baby. I'd hate for him to be born into this world like his step mommy."

"What are you talking about?" she asked with an uninterested look on her face.

"I'm so glad you asked," she said, throwing a pill bottle on the table near Jaxon.

"Truvada? What is this?" he asked, picking the bottle up to read the label.

Chey knew exactly what it was because Von took the same medicine.

"It's used to treat HIV/AIDS," she said as Zaria took the

3

whole bottle of Hennessey to the head.

The way everyone's hearts dropped into their stomachs was equivalent to a meteor falling from the sky into the ocean. The results would be catastrophic and that was exactly how everyone in that room was feeling.

"Ma? What are you saying?" Qyree asked. Even though he had heard her clearly just like everybody else, he was praying his ears were deceiving him the same way his father had. If hearing that he had a brother that was taking over his spot in the company wasn't enough to send him over the edge, then finding out his mother had a deadly disease was about to do the trick. Not even the fact that Natalia was trying to pin her unborn baby on him, moved him to tears, but this sure did.

"Baby," Zaria began as she walked over to Qyree. The closer she got to him, the further back he moved out of her reach. Seeing that he was not about to let her get near him, she stood where she was and did her best to comfort him. "I'm sorry you had to find out this way, Qy. I never meant to hurt you. I tried so many times to tell you but I didn't know how. I knew it would disrupt your life the longer I waited, but I wanted you to be happy and focus on your career. Once

4

I started finding out information about what Jaxon was doing and who he was doing it with, I knew I had to tell you," she explained.

"Don't listen to your mother! She's drunk and talking out the side of her face right now. This is just like you, Zaria, to want everything to be about you," Jaxon fumed. He may have been putting up a front on the outside, but internally he was a nervous wreck. After all of the years he had been doing his dirt, now it was coming back to bite him in his behind.

He knew that what his grandmother used to tell him was indeed true, and he had failed at hearing her warnings. She would always tell him at a young age that what you sow you shall also reap. No matter if you sow a good seed or a bad one, one day that harvest would be ready to be harvested and you would have to deal with it.

Was he sick too? Nah, couldn't be. He didn't look sick and he felt better than he had in years. Young women would do that to him, though, he thought to himself, causing a smirk to adorn his face.

"This is funny to you?" Qy raised his voice, noticing the

5

look on his father's face. Jaxon hadn't realized he was smiling until that moment.

"Nah, not funny. It's hysterical! You want me to sit up here and believe that your mother caught one of the most diseases in the world from me? I'm not sick. Get the—" he started, only to be cut off with a slap to the face. Zaria had crossed over to his side of the room so fast, no one had time to stop her from slapping the taste out of his mouth.

"You no good bastard! I'm counting down the days until I leave this earth and you want to stand over here smiling, thinking this is a game! My mother told me that one day you would be the death of me, and now I understand what she meant," she yelled in his face. "I swear I hope that old shriveled up hell between your thighs falls off, you son of a—
"

"MA!" Qyree yelled out to his mother. He knew she was about to go off the deep end by the way her breathing had picked up and because he noticed her fists were balled up at her sides. He couldn't blame her for how she felt and her actions would be justified. He just didn't want his mother to have to go any further outside of her character, so he had to stop her before she went too far out there.

Not turning to acknowledge her son or anyone else in the room, she simply walked over to one of the drawers in the cabinets and pulled out some papers.

"Here," she said shoving them in Jaxon's face.

"What is this?" he asked her.

"Oh, just a dose of reality for that behind!" she said, waiting for him to read what was on the papers.

For over a year, Zaria had been living with the virus and just recently her doctors discovered it had turned into full blown AIDS. The results of her last tests months ago confirmed that it was progressing extremely fast, and that was the day she began drinking heavier than she ever had in her life. She felt like if she stayed drunk constantly, the pain and revelation would go away. Qyree and Jaxon may have thought she was heavy on the bottle because of what he was doing, but it was so much more than that.

Jaxon studied the dates that was on the papers and like clockwork, Zaria knew exactly what he was thinking.

"Yup. I got tested last year, a week after I caught you with this trick in my house, yet again, and got the results

7

shortly after. I knew that if you were sleeping with her, I better get checked 'cause word on the streets was that she had it," she said, turning up the bottle once again.

No one spoke a word for what seemed like forever, not even Toni, until Natalia opened her mouth.

"Oh my God," she said looking flushed in the face.

"Girl, God don't even like you so stop calling Him like you know Him," Zaria snapped.

Ignoring her petty remark, Natalia grabbed at her stomach and moaned. It was at that moment that they saw the water trickling down her legs and on to the floor.

"I know this girl did not just break her water on my good floor," Zaria said, peering over the top of the table.

"Qy, please take me to the hospital," Natalia said. The smirk was evident on her face and she just knew that she had one up on Chey.

"Why would I take you?" he asked unmoved.

"Because this is your child just as much as it is mine!" she started yelling before the crocodile tears made their way

down her face.

Chey just stood there and looked at the woman she used to call her friend and felt not one ounce of remorse for her. She knew it was wrong and would more than likely repent later for her thoughts, but right then it wasn't happening. Natalia brought this on herself and instead of worrying about the health of her unborn baby, she was worried about a man. Typical Natalia.

"You know that's not my baby, man. Maybe my brother or sister, but definitely not my child. You got me messed up," he told her confidently. He could never deny the fact that he slept with Natalia, although he wished he could, but he wouldn't. If he was man enough to smash, he was man enough to say he did. But one thing he learned a long time ago from his father was to always wear protection. That was the only good thing that Jaxon had done for his son, and it was on a technicality.

Before Qyree had become sexually active, there had been at least three women claiming that Jaxon was the father of their babies. It was then that he knew he had to strap up. He wasn't even thinking about catching anything, he was focused on not having babies all over the world.

9

"OOMPH," Natalia bent over in pain. The look on everyone's faces were looks of being unbothered. All except one.

Running up to her, he caught her just in time before she hit the floor just as another contraction hit.

"JJ, what are you doing?" Toni asked her son.

"I can't let my son be born on this floor. I gotta get her to the hospital," he said helping Natalia get to the door.

"Wow," was all Chey and Qyree could say when that bomb dropped.

"Ha! Baby, forget that lemonade Beyoncé poured. You got to get you some of this here Jack Daniels being sipped on up in here!" Zaria laughed as she cracked the top on a new bottle and took it to the head.

-2-

Qyree sat in his office thinking of his life and the direction that he was going in. Just when he thought that everything was lining up the right way, he started to get hit from all sides. It was like he had finally found the woman that challenged him to be better and she was always so positive. It was crazy though, as he was becoming a successful A&R getting ready to take over that division of his father's company one minute, the next he was finding out how ruthless life could be.

He should have been really enjoying this season of his life but he wasn't. Chey had even helped him turn back to God and rededicate his life to Christ, but it felt like once he did that, his life started to go on a downward hill. He understood that once he made that decision to live right he would be attacked even harder, and it almost caused him to turn back to his old ways, but once again there Chey was, helping him to remain strong.

Chey... his strength in the flesh. He knew the first time

he set his eyes on her that she was the one, but he also knew that he wasn't ready to be tied down to just one woman. When they went their separate ways, he focused his thoughts elsewhere but when they saw each other again, he knew that was God. She made him work for her love and that was new to him. He never had to work hard when it came to other women, and he should have known then that they weren't about anything. Qyree knew now that a woman who didn't value or love herself or her body wasn't one that he wanted to be linked up with. No one was perfect in the least and everyone fell short of the glory of God, but he understood a little better what he needed to change in his life before he could expect to be what his future wife needed. That's why he had to let Chey go.

Before he could dwell on that situation any longer than he needed to, there was a knock at his door.

"Come in," he said as he tugged on his beard. He would always do that when he was stressed and his thoughts were everywhere.

"What's good, bruh?" Tank asked coming into the room.

Tank, whose real name was Channing, was Qyree's first

12

cousin on his father's side. Growing up, they were as thick as thieves and acted more like brothers than cousins. Once they graduated, Qyree went off to college and Channing decided to go into the military. He would have still been in had he not gotten out on a medical discharge. Because it was an honorable discharge, he was able to keep his benefits from Uncle Sam. He used that to buy himself a house back home in Stockbridge and saved the rest that he received in his monthly benefits.

Considering the fact that they always wanted to be in the music business together and Qyree was finally free of Satan aka Jaxon, this was the perfect opportunity for them to do it together. As long as Qy was still under his father, Tank wanted nothing to do with the business because he couldn't stand his uncle. Not only did his influence mess up Qy's way of thinking when it came to the women, it messed Tank's up as well.

Because he had gotten his nickname when the singer Tank came out on the scene, he used that and his teachings to get the women that he wanted in his bed. Channing "Tank" Watkins knew he was that dude in the looks department. Standing at 6'3", he had that football player build that drove the ladies crazy. He hadn't played one quarter of the game in his life, but they didn't care. His Hennessey colored skin was covered in tattoos, he kept his hair cut low and tapered on the sides, and the hair on his face was thick but neatly trimmed. That was the only difference between him and the singer.

"Can't call it," Qyree responded, still in his thoughts a little.

"Still haven't talked to her?" Tank asked as he made his way over to the chair that sat in front of Qyree's desk. Instead of responding verbally, Qy just shook his head solemnly.

The two of them were quiet for a few minutes before Tank spoke again.

"Aye, you remember that time in second grade when Brandi stabbed me in the hand with that pencil for no reason?" he asked, thinking back on their childhood.

"Man, go 'head. You know she had a reason. You pushed that girl out of her chair 'cause she told you that your color by numbers sheet was ugly," Qy laughed, remembering the incident well. Tank thought that she was going to run and tell the teacher and he wasn't prepared for the G to come out of

14

her. As soon as she got up off the floor, she reached for her pencil and stabbed him dead in the hand he was coloring with, then called him a punk.

"Anyway, you remember what you told me?"

"I told you to stop acting like a little girl with all that crying."

"Not that part, dummy. The part where you told me that I should apologize and let her know that I was wrong."

"Yea, she still curved you every chance she got," he laughed again. "What made you think of that?"

"I just think that you need to apologize to Chey and make it right. I know I haven't gotten the chance to meet her in person just yet, but I can tell she was good for you. You changed but it's been for the better. Don't make her feel like this is her fault because when you go back and try to fix it, it might be too late."

"Who said I was blaming her? What my family had going on isn't her fault," Qy said, frowning up his face.

"So why did you let her go?" Tank wanted to know.

Qy just stared at his cousin, not having a valid answer. Every reason he came up with when he thought about it on his own, wasn't a good one. He just thought she would be better off without him but he didn't know why.

"Make it right, cuz. If you need me to go with you to holla at her, just hit me up," Tank said, rising from his chair and leaving Qyree to himself.

-3-

"They tell me 'Zari, you know you work too hard'. But I tell them not nearly hard enough. Heyyy, you and those Pips better sang Gladys!" Zaria incorrectly sang as she danced around her room packing. She had a few shirts in her left hand as she turned up her bottle of alcohol with her right.

"So you destroy everyone's worlds and you're in here singing and dancing like it's a celebration?" she heard Jaxon say behind her.

Not feeling one ounce of remorse, she turned around to face the man that had thrown her love overboard years ago. Looking at him from head to toe, Jaxon was still the most handsome man to her on the outside, but his insides were uglier than she had ever imagined a person could be. The man standing before her was not the man she had shared vows with in front of God and almost a hundred of their friends all of those years prior. No, this man was evil and took not only her love for him, but their son's love for his father for granted. She could care less how he felt about her

17

revealing the death sentence he gave her.

"You doggone right it's a celebration. A celebration of me finally getting back at you and getting rid of your trifling behind!" she yelled, getting in his face. The mixture of saliva and vodka that remained in her mouth, sprayed on him like a light mist.

Wiping his face, he looked at his wife with as much hatred as he could muster up, letting her know that she was about to be caught up in his line of fire. It had been years since he put his hands on her, but she was pushing him to go back to his old ways.

"I'm warning you Zaria," he said in an icy tone while wiping his face.

Unmoved and unbothered with her "Resting Zaria" face, she moved closer to him with a smirk on her beautiful chocolate face.

"What, you need to get in a few punches? Go ahead and give it your best shot and when you're done slapping me around and choking me out, make sure you lock the door behind you," she said, walking back over to her dresser where she had set her bottle down. Just as soon as she got the rim to her mouth, it was snatched out of her hand and went crashing to the wall.

"I know you didn't, you bas—" Zaria started as she charged at Jaxon with everything her little drunk body had in her. She moved so fast that he didn't have time to protect his face, and the blow that cut off her sentence landed right in his jaw.

Jaxon was a big man and he knew that Zaria had to have been drunk to hit him that hard. He was a little dazed for a few seconds as she landed a left after the right. Before he had enough time to grab her and let her have it, he felt her being lifted off of him.

"GET OFF OF ME! GET OFF OF ME!" she yelled as Qyree held her tight. He had come over because his life was spiraling out of control and he needed to talk to his mother. After the conversation that he had with Tank, he knew he needed to go and see her. No matter what she had gone through or had done, he still loved her and needed her. He wasn't too sure how much encouragement she could give him considering her own mental state, but she had never led him wrong before. He just never chose to walk the path she was trying to lead him to. Instead, he chose to follow a man

19

that meant him nor his mother any good.

"You need to leave," Qyree said as calmly as he could. The anger and rage that he felt when he saw his father's car in the driveway when he pulled up was threatening to boil over at that very moment, and he prayed that Jaxon would leave before it did.

Qyree and Jaxon hadn't seen one another since the night all of the secrets were revealed, and if he never would see his father for the rest of his life after that, it would still be too soon. He hadn't been home to see his mama since the incident, but he still talked to her every day. She had told him that Jaxon had moved out and hadn't been back, so to see him there this day was an unwelcomed sight.

"This is my house!" Jaxon said getting even more upset. He didn't care what he had done, it was his hard earned money that paid for this lifestyle and he could be there if he wanted to be. The only reason he left in the first place was because he knew that if he had stayed, he would probably be in jail by now.

For Zaria to say that he had given her a sexually transmitted disease was a low blow. She was far from innocent like she pretended to be. Well at least that was what he kept telling himself to justify his actions. After all of these years, no one could tell him that she knew he was stepping out on her and she didn't do the same to get back at him. Nah, she got that from one of her jump-offs and nothing could be said to tell him otherwise.

Both Zaria and Qy glared at Jaxon with the same hate filled look etched across their faces. Qy was still holding his mother around her waist so she couldn't get to Jaxon, and if he continued to just stand there instead of leaving, he was going to let her go. Although Jaxon used to beat on Zaria, she had never just sat there and took it. She would always fight back and she didn't fight fair either. Whatever was in her reach, she would pick it up and use as her weapon of choice.

None of them would ever forget the time they were going at it and she picked up a curling iron that she was using at the time and pressed it against his face. She was in the bathroom curling her hair when they started arguing about one of his many flings. Jaxon felt like she had been nagging him and he couldn't take it anymore. He burst into the bathroom and punched her in the back of her head as hard as he could. Without missing a beat, she turned around and pressed the hot iron against the left side of his face. Qy ran into the room screaming and crying and that's when they stopped. Most people would think they wouldn't travel down that abusive road again after he witnessed them fighting, or that Zaria would leave, but neither happened.

Qyree, for the life of him, still didn't understand why his mother would take all of the abuse that she did. From the cheating, to the physical altercations, to the emotional and mental abuse, she took it all. For him, his mother was the poster child for women who didn't know their worth, but that was still his mother and he loved her.

"You have a week to be out of my house," he said to her.

"I'm not going anywhere," Zaria slurred.

Shrugging his shoulders and putting his hands in his pockets as he moved towards the door, he looked at them and spoke.

"Either you leave willingly or get carried out. The choice is yours," he said in a menacing voice and then walked out.

The tone of his voice let Qyree and Zaria know that he

22

meant every word that had just come out of his mouth. He may have hit her, but never had he threatened to take her life. The devil himself had taken over Jaxon, and Zaria was not about to stick around to have him make good on his promise.

She may have already been dying, but the last thing she wanted was to speed up the process. He wanted her gone then he could consider it done. But not before she made him pay for the hell on earth he caused her.

-4-

"Mommy, don't forget my field trip money, ok?" Amir said, reminding his mother of his upcoming trip to the zoo.

"I won't baby," she smiled at him before he leaned over and kissed her on her cheek before jumping out of the car and running towards the school.

If anyone had told her a year ago that she would be living a normal and happy life with her son, she would have called them a liar. God had really blessed her in spite of her past actions and she would be forever thankful to Him. No one could convince her that God was not real because He had brought her a mighty long way, even when she didn't deserve it.

Amir turned around one last time before walking through the doors of the school and waved at her before she pulled off. Being able to take him to school and provide for him was a dream come true. At first she thought that he wouldn't want anything to do with her and would choose to stay in

Florida with Nivea and Terrance. She wouldn't have blamed him if he did because that was the only life he had known. So the day that she received a call from Nivea letting her know that he wanted to come and stay with her, she was ecstatic.

With the help of Chey, she was able to get her a nice little spot to live in, a car, and even a good steady job. Because she was studying to become a counselor, Chey was able to pull a few strings to get her a full-time position at the local clinic. She was paid well, but once she got her degree, she would get a raise that would really have her and Amir set up nice.

Thinking of Chey made her not only think about how much of a blessing she was to her, but Von also thought about Chey's situation with Qyree. She knew that Qyree never wanted to hurt Chey, but he didn't know how to handle everything that was going on in his life and Chey was taking it so hard. Chey was one of the strongest women that she had come to know and she looked up to her, so seeing her in the state she had been in lately was hard for her as well. That's why she took it upon herself to help fix it.

It was early and she didn't have to go to work until after

lunchtime, so she made her way into Huddle House in search of her party. Taking a few minutes to observe the room, her eyes landed on Qyree. Since the hostess was nowhere to be found, she took it upon herself to seat herself at his table.

"Hey Qy," she said as he stood up to greet her. He gave her a tight hug before pulling her seat out so that she could sit down.

"I hope you don't mind, but I brought my cousin Tank along with me," he told her with a weary look in his eyes. Von felt so bad for him and she prayed that this would be the beginning of her friends getting back on the right track. Before she could let him know that she was cool with his cousin being there and asking where he was, she heard one of the smoothest voices she had ever heard in her life.

"Man, that Buffalo Wild Wings from last night doing a number on your boy," Tank said before realizing Qyree wasn't alone. "My bad, love."

Von felt like her words were caught in her throat and what she was thinking to say just wasn't coming out. If there was a justice of the peace in that place at that moment, she would have kindly asked him to marry the two of them.

Qyree was fine but his cousin was a masterpiece.

"Sis, this is my cousin, Channing, and cuz, this is Von," Qy introduced them. The way they were both staring into each other's souls, he knew that he had to be the one to break the ice.

"Um, nice to meet you," Von said, clearing her throat.

"The pleasure is all mine, beautiful," Tank said to her.

"Has anyone ever told you how much you look like Tank, the R&B singer?" she asked, mesmerized.

"All the time. That's how I got the nickname Tank," he smiled, causing her to feel like she was melting in her seat.

Von watched the way that Tank moved around as if he owned the air that she was breathing. That didn't make any sense to her, but that was just the way she was feeling. Taking a second to get her mind right, she began to thank God for him choosing to sit on the other side of the table. Had he sat next to her, she was sure she was going to end up in that man's lap.

"God forgive me," she said to herself.

"He will," Tank said and smiled at her. Von was sure she had died and her spirit was tootsie rolling to heaven when she realized that she had spoken out loud.

"So what's good, sis?" Qyree asked, bringing her back to why she was there.

"It's Chey," she began, only to be cut off by him.

"Is she ok?" he asked. The look on his face let her know that the love hadn't faded and that she was still his main concern.

"Physically, she's fine, but emotionally she's a wreck, Qy. I've done my best to talk to her and cheer her up, but nothing is working. Why haven't you reached out to her?"

Qy knew that ending things with her was the best thing for her. Well, that's what he felt in the beginning anyway. As the seconds turned to minutes, minutes to hours, and hours to days, he started to seriously doubt his actions. It wasn't her fault that his family was in shambles but if he had to be honest with himself, he would say that his issue wasn't even really with them but himself. Qyree had done something that he knew he shouldn't have and to acknowledge it scared him.

28

Grabbing at his beard, he sat back in his chair not sure how he wanted to answer this line of questioning. He could see the desperation on Von's face and hear it in her voice, and just like him, he knew that she loved Chey and would do anything to help her through this rough patch.

"It's complicated," he simply said.

"Well give it to me Barney style then," she said crossing her arms and sitting back in her chair as the waiter walked up to the table.

"My name is Earnest and I will be your server today. Can I start you off with something to drink?" he asked, but only looked at Von when he spoke.

"I'll take a Coke and some hot wings off the appetizers list," Tank jumped in.

The way his face was slightly balled up surprised Von, and she was even flattered. She knew he was feeling some type of way about the way Earnest was looking at her, and it gave her butterflies. It was a feeling that had been so foreign to her for years now and it had suddenly returned, and it made her feel excited. That was until she thought about her condition.

She knew that she had no one to blame but herself for her wild and careless ways, and how she treated those who loved her when she was younger, and she had long ago accepted her fate. It didn't mean, though, that she didn't want to experience a happily ever after with a husband and her son. She wanted to have that family that she grew up around with Nivea and her grandparents, the marriage that Nivea now had with Terrance, and even the relationship that she saw blossom between Chey and Qyree.

"And for you, beautiful?" Earnest smiled politely. He could already feel the vibe from the dude who rudely interrupted him with his order. But considering the fact that they didn't look to be together in any way, he decided to try his luck.

"Um, actually, I'll have the same thing," she said. For some reason the way he looked at her made Von uncomfortable, and the sooner he got away from the table and her, the better she would feel.

"And you, sir?" he asked Qy.

"I'm straight," was all he said as the waiter turned to walk away. He hadn't really had an appetite in a while and

30

just hearing how bad off Chey was because of him, made it go away once again.

Focusing back on Qy and avoiding the glare that she felt from Tank, she went back to the question that she had originally asked.

"So why is it complicated?"

Once again, before she could get the answer she was seeking, they were interrupted. This time due to Qyree's phone ringing in his pocket. He had been waiting all day for a specific call and without looking at the screen, he excused himself and walked out of the restaurant, leaving Von and Tank alone.

"Don't worry, I won't bite," he told Von as she giggled.

"I bet. So why haven't we met before?" she wanted to know. It had been going on a year since she met Qy and never once had Tank been around them and he was never mentioned either.

"I just got back into town. I'm recently retired from the military and decided to come and help my cousin run his new company. This had been one of our dreams when we were younger but once he went off to college to get his degree, I decided to join the Navy," he explained.

"Oh, ok. Did you like it?"

"Man, I loved the Navy. Getting to travel the world and see so many different things was amazing. Especially being able to walk the path that Jesus walked in the Holy Land," he said, smiling. Von could tell that the experience meant a lot to him and that was once place that she had always dreamed of going.

"I know that had to have been powerful. When I was younger, I wasn't really trying to have a relationship with God. Well, not a real one at least. I knew who He was but I made no attempt to really get close until a few years ago. Now that I have, one of my dreams is to take a trip there and experience that tour. I want my son to be able to have that memory with me since we have missed so much time together. That would be a memory that neither of us would ever forget."

"If you don't mind me asking, why have you missed time with him? Was he with his father or something?" Tank wanted to know as he took a bite of his wing. He didn't want

32

her to think he was prying or being too pushy, but he was honestly interested in her and finding out she had a son let him know they were a package deal. He didn't have any kids of his own and more than likely never would, so getting to know the two of them would be a blessing.

"No, I don't mind talking about it. I've gotten to a place in life where I'm no longer ashamed of my past because it made me the woman that I am today. I was sentenced to four years in jail back when I was seventeen, for setting up my best friend to get hurt. I just didn't expect her to get hurt so badly, and I regret my part in it. I should have been released on my twenty-first birthday, but I kept getting in trouble so time was added. At the time I hadn't yet come to terms that the reason I was there was because of my actions. I blamed everyone around me and felt like me showing out and behaving badly was the answer. Not even realizing that it really wasn't.

When I got locked up, I didn't know that I was pregnant. It wasn't until after I received information that I had contracted HIV that the jail took me for a health screening and I found out that I was expecting. That was when I really began to show out. Fighting other inmates, bucking back at

33

the guards and the warden, just real grimy stuff. Then one day I felt my baby kick and it was as if Amir was asking me to stop. I didn't turn around completely right then but I did slow down," Von expressed to him. She was waiting on him to show a sign of disgust or hate for what she had just told him, but she found neither. For a second, she thought she saw a look of admiration flicker in his eyes, but that quickly left.

"We all fall short of the glory of God daily, but we have to make sure that we keep pressing towards Him. Our end is greater than our beginning and the reward is better than one we could ever imagine. I've made too many mistakes to count, and some I'm still paying for to this second, but I won't let the enemy use those mistakes to make me quit. Does he try to keep reminding me of my past and who I was? Every chance he gets. But I know his future, and every time he reminds me I remind him right back. Anyway, hopefully we can get these two love birds back together and I can get to know you a little better, along with your son," Tank said, surprising her. Never had she met a man that was willing to continue to talk to her after—not only telling him she had a child—but that she was HIV positive. All she could do was

34

smile and nod her head in response to him, before taking a bite of her own food.

Sitting in silence a few more minutes as they ate, both Von and Tank were deep in their thoughts about their conversation as Qyree finally made his way back to the table. The look on his face told them that something was seriously wrong and he looked defeated.

"Aye you alright, bruh?" Tank asked, noticing his demeanor.

"The first call I got was from this producer cat I was waiting to hear back from. One of the hottest in the business. He's just starting out but he's making some serious noise right now and I want him on our team before someone else has a chance to snatch him up," Qy said, knowing exactly who the 'someone' he was referring to was Jaxon, who also wanted to work with the producer.

"Yo! I know you not talking about Anointed One," Tank said excitedly, as he balled his fist up and covered his mouth with it.

"The one and only," Qy told him, but he looked far from happy about it.

"So what's good? Y'all gonna link up and get this ball rolling or what?"

Von just sat there taking in everything she was hearing and she wanted to be so excited for Qy, but the way he was looking had her holding off on her celebration. Something wasn't right and she had wished that Chey was here to comfort the almost broken man that sat in front of her.

"I would definitely be ready to put in work if I had somewhere to put in work at."

"What you mean? I know the studio not complete yet, but you can still get things going so when it is, y'all will already be ahead of the game," Tank encouraged. Qy was talking in riddles and it was beginning to make him worry. If anyone knew how to make things work it was Qyree, so him sounding like he was at a loss was new to him.

"While I was talking to AO, another call came through but I didn't answer right away because I didn't know the number, and linking up with him was more important. Just as we finished our convo, the same number called back and this time I answered. It was a fire marshal telling me that my studio had been burned to the ground."

"Oh my God, Qy!" Von said as tears formed in her eyes. She knew how much this meant to Qyree and how hard he worked to get to this point only for it to be snatched away from him.

"Yo, stop playin', bruh. Are you serious?" Tank asked. He could feel the pain that his cousin was feeling but something wasn't right about this.

"I wish I was, man. God knows I do," Qy sighed.

"But how did it catch on fire? It couldn't have been electrical because the wiring hadn't been done yet," Tank stated. It was as if a light went off in his head at that moment.

Qy had been so upset about the fact that his dream burned down to the ground that he didn't even think to ask how it all started. The only thing the marshal told him was that he would be in touch and it was under investigation.

Tank looked at Qy and it was like they both thought the same thing at the same time. Both men were almost positive that they knew who was behind the fire and it was confirmed when they opened their mouths simultaneously to speak.

"Jaxon."

"Wait a minute. You think your father did this? I know I
have heard the stories of how he is, but do you really think
he would stoop this far to hurt you? He's caused enough
damage to your family already," Von said, looking from Qy
to Tank, hoping that one of them would tell her that they
were just playing, but neither did.

"Sis, there is so much evil in that man that I'm not sure if
he is capable of caring about anyone else's feelings. If he
did, he may just burst in to flames. Ay, but don't tell Chey
about this. I know if she knew then she would try to come
around and be here for me and I just can't do that right now,
aight?" Qy said. As bad as she wanted to tell Chey, the only
reason she would respect his wishes this time was because
she knew that in her condition, she didn't need the added
stress. Von was doing her best to get her out of her funk, and
hearing this bit of news, she knew that it would make things
worse.

"I won't. Besides, she doesn't need this added on to
everything else she is going through," Von told him, getting
up from her seat. As soon as the words left her mouth she
regretted it, and prayed that Qy would just let it ride, but it

38

was just her luck that he didn't.

"What you mean everything else? She alright?" he asked with a worried expression on his face.

Von thought that maybe if she told him the truth that he would go and see her and they could work things out, considering they had to be in one another's presence. But then again, it could backfire and cause more problems than anything. That was just a chance she wasn't willing to take.

"She's fine. Um, I meant with everything going on with the two of you and work, that's all. Hey, look, I have to go pay for Amir's field trip before noon so I should be getting out of here. It was nice meeting you, Tank," she said hurriedly.

"The pleasure was all mine," he smiled back as she took off towards the front. Had she taken another minute to stand there, she would be spilling tea and passing out crumpets. The last thing she wanted to do was overstep her boundaries and intrude on their relationship, so she would just pray that God would make everything right so that things could stop going so wrong.

-5-

Twenty minutes had gone by as they drove before either
Qy or Tank said a word to one another. Each man was deep
in his own thoughts. Qy was trying to let the anger subside
about his father stooping to an all-time low just to make his
life a living hell, and Tank's mind was on Von. In just that
short amount of time, that woman had his mind gone and he
wished he had just a little more time to get to hang with her.
He knew that Qy may look at him crazy about getting her
information, but it was now or never.

"So what's up with Miss Von? She taken?" Tank asked
after leaning over and turning down the radio.

Glancing over at his cousin, Qy couldn't help but to
crack a slight smile. He knew from the time that Tank and
Von met they were feeling each other, because their eyes
told it on them straight from the jump. He just didn't know
how Tank would take the information of her having a son
and her health condition. If the son didn't turn him away,
then he was sure that her illness would. He wouldn't blame

him though, but Von was now family and the last thing he wanted was for her to get hurt in the process. Tank was a good man, but he, too, had his ways.

"Nah, she not taken, but I think you should keep it moving," Qy honestly told him. He didn't want to be the one to tell Tank why they couldn't be together, so he hoped he would drop it.

"If you're worried that I would hurt her because of her son or the fact that she has HIV, you can stop worrying. I may have had my share of women and done my dirt in my day, but I would never intentionally hurt someone like that," he told Qy, shocking him.

"She told you?"

"Yea. She put it all out there and that just made me respect her more. How often do you find a woman that is willing to be totally honest and up front? Man, most of the time they lying about small stuff like having a head full of hair and being born with those tiny waists. Knowing good and well they got both the hair and those waist things off of Ali Express or Instagram."

Qy thought he was about to pass out from laughing so

41

hard. Leave it up to Tank, to act just like he used to do in the old times, to make him laugh and for a moment, he stopped him from thinking about his problems. There was only one other person that could ease his mind, but he had made sure to block her out. So right now Tank would have to do.

"Bruh, you wild, man," Qy continued to laugh.

"I'm dead serious. I remember one time I went back to this chick's spot that I had met in the club. Man, she was about to be my baby mama on life! Body was bangin', she smelled good, and she lived in a good neighborhood. Come to find out she was a RN at one of the local hospitals down in Jacksonville. We had stopped through there on one of our deployments.

Anyway, we get back to her crib or whatever and ya boy is in awe. Most of the chicks I dealt with either lived with their mama and siblings at her Big Mama's house, or somewhere that only charged her to pay $3.50 in rent. Don't get me wrong, ain't nothing wrong with that. Shoot, I wish my rent was $3.50. I'm paying that up for at least ten years," Tank laughed.

Qy couldn't help but to laugh harder because Tank was

getting hype telling his story and cracking jokes all the way through.

"So her house was decked out and clean as a whistle. Lil' mama got me all relaxed and said that she was going to go slip into something more comfortable. That's how they say they 'bout to give you some without sounding like they be out there. Ole girl went in looking like Miss America and came out looking like Old Otis the security guard! I mean nappy 'fro and all. I was like 'Aye bruh, I ain't know she had a dude, she told me she was single, straight up!' and she had the nerve to catch an attitude. Tawm 'bout I was being funny and I was acting like a typical man who was caught up on just looks. I told her, 'Look bruh, I ain't sign up for this. At least let the bedroom action be so good that it don't matter what you look like so I have no choice but to come back.' She ain't give ya boy nothing, for real for real!"

"My dude, you stupid!" Qyree yelled out. He was trying so hard to catch his breath and stop the tears from falling, but Tank just wouldn't shut up and his story kept getting funnier and funnier. If he didn't regain his composure, he was going to have to pull over until he got it together. The last thing he needed to do was run off the road 'cause he couldn't stop laughing at the fool in his passenger seat.

Once they were both able to gather themselves, Tank got serious again. He had yet to fill Qy in on everything that had gone on with him recently, and he knew when he did, then maybe he would understand why he felt the way that he did towards Von.

"The reason I wasn't thrown off by what Von told me about her condition is because we are one in the same," he told his cousin. Not many people knew that this was the reason that he was medically discharged from the military and unlike Von, he wasn't at the place yet where he could freely divulge that bit of information to just anyone. Of course he was able to deal with it a little better than he had when he first found out, but there were some days it was still tough. He saw how others who lived with it were looked down upon, and he just didn't want to get the same reaction from people. It was like once they knew, they treated you like you were the scum of the earth and no matter how tough he was; it still stung a bit.

"Yo, you serious?" Qy wondered. This had to be some sick joke because the man that had grown up with him his whole life, was sitting next to him looking like he had never

44

even had a cold in his life. His body looked like he lived in a gym, his skin was blemish free, and he didn't lose any weight. By looking at his mother and Von, you couldn't tell that they had it either, but this was just too much to take in all at once.

"This is the seed that I sowed so long ago and now I'm having to reap the harvest. My wild and fun days have turned into a many sad and lonely nights with the realization that I may never have that chance at having a family because of me being positive. It's tough, but I have to deal with it."

"I'm sorry, bruh. I can't even imagine what you gotta be going through," Qy told him. He had been scared to go and test himself after hearing that his mother had contracted the disease and Natalia was sleeping with his father. But he knew that he couldn't risk putting someone else at risk, especially Chey. He put a rush order on the test and was told that in another six months he would need to come back and test again, but so far he was negative and he had no one to thank but God. Just like his cousin, he was out there living reckless to an extent because he always strapped up, but nothing was a hundred percent but being abstinent, so he was still taking chances.

"That's why you gotta make things right with Chey," Tank said, bringing him from his thoughts.

"What does she have to do with this? Me staying away, is protecting her from further heartbreak."

"You don't think her heart is breaking now? The one man that she thought was going to be there just up and left her, and for what? From what you told me, she was even leery about starting something with you because she didn't want to be hurt, and here you are doing the exact same thing she feared. We go way back, bruh, and you know I have seen you around plenty broads. She's the one and you need to fix it before it's too late."

As stubborn as Qy was, he knew that Tank was right about everything he had just said. Not too many people these days would tell someone what they needed to hear; they were too busy worrying about being liked by that person. Those who claimed to be 'A-ones since day one' would just tell you want you wanted to hear and when that advice would backfire, they would laugh behind your back. That's why Qy was blessed to have Tank and Chey in his life. Neither of them cared nothing about him liking what they had to say if it was something that could help him. In the long run, each time they would end up right.

Even his mother had tried plenty of times to tell him to stop treating women the way he was and to change his perception on how he treated them, but he didn't listen. All he saw was that the same thing that she was telling him to stop dishing out to women, were the same things she was taking from his own father. He needed to see results and Jaxon was the one who gave it to him. The way the women responded to Jaxon when he applied those same teachings he was giving to Qy, made him want to follow behind his father even more. He now understood though, that if God hadn't opened his eyes, he would be following his father right to hell.

-6-

This was the last place that Natalia wanted to return to, but since her most recent plan of trapping one of the Reeves men backfired, she had no choice. Pulling her car into the driveway of her grandparents' home brought back so many good memories. Then again, it also brought back quite a few bad ones, but those were the ones she caused herself.

Natalia's grandparents, Pastor Cecil and First Lady Gladys Fonville, were two of the most respected people in their hometown of Valdosta. They had lived there for over fifty years and were the epitome of great leaders in their community. They had raised all three of their children, including Natalia's mother Leticia, to be God fearing and productive citizens, but those values seemed to skip Leticia. She was their wild child and bucked against everything that they had tried to instill in her. They would always find her getting into something that ended up getting her in trouble, until one day it took her life.

With Natalia being their only grandchild, they wanted to

48

do all that they could to prevent her from going down that same road, but the harder they tried, the more she bucked against them. For a long time, they didn't have any issues with her. She would enjoy going to church, had good grades, and was always a respectable young lady. The friendship that she had formed with Chey, they trusted would be beneficial in Natalia being a productive citizen. The two of them were inseparable and although they had similarities, there were also many differences between them. Then one day it seemed as if everything just began to make a turn for the worse. Natalia started getting into fights, skipping school, playing around when it came time to go to church, just anything that she could do to have all the attention on her.

Cecil was either blind to the situation or he just chose not to say anything, but Gladys on the other hand saw right through her. She knew the moment when the changes started to appear in her grandchild that she was smelling herself. Some little boy had made his way into her life and she thought she knew everything. After years of trying to get her on the right track, Gladys had had enough. She politely packed up everything that Natalia had bought, which was only a bag of tampons and a head scarf, and sent her on her way. The tender love they were trying to give her wasn't received, so tough love had to be put in to place.

The moment she got up to the front door with her son's car seat in hand, she was reminded of the many reasons tough love had to be used and if she could, she would take back every single thing she had done in her past. At that moment, she couldn't understand how some people could say that they had no regrets in life, because she had more than she could count. She wanted so bad to pray, but she felt like God was so far away from her, so there was no use to do it. It was too late now and everything Cecil and Gladys tried to warn her about couldn't be undone.

Natalia rang the doorbell and waited. Looking down into her son's handsome face as he began to wake up made her happy and sad at the same time. Happy because of the life she created but sad because their life would never be normal as she had planned. Money wouldn't be an issue but everything else would be. She knew that once the door in front of her opened, judgment would be on the other side of it so she braced herself.

"Hey Poppa," she smiled weakly at her grandfather.

Cecil Fonville was a tall old man. He stood about six foot three and had a complexion that resembled the color of an almond. His silver hair was cut low, as usual, and he wore one of those linen outfits that seemed like all preachers and pastors wore; the button down short sleeve shirt with the pants to match. If you wore one of those out in public, nine times out of ten, people could tell exactly what you did for a living.

The crow's feet near both of his auburn colored eyes were due to stress, and Natalia knew that was partially her fault. Looking at him, she wanted so much to run into his open arms and have him take away everything that she was going through, but the look on his face prevented that. He didn't look mad, but he didn't look happy to see her either. Following his eyes to the ground beside her, he studied her son's face as his shoulders slumped and his eyes began to water. There was no doubt in her mind about what he was thinking and that was one of the reasons they had no clue about her son.

"Who is that at the door, Cecil?" she heard her grandmother yell, and she immediately cringed. Not because she hated Gladys, but because she knew that any moment she

51

would be ripped a new one.

Ignoring the question, Cecil reached out with his left hand to grab the car seat and with his right, he reached for Natalia. All he could do was offer her a small smile, hoping that gave her some kind of comfort for what she was walking in to. He knew that if she had showed up here, it was because she had hit rock bottom, and Gladys was not about to go easy on her. Cecil had been watching Natalia as soon as she pulled into the yard, from his living room window, and was able to prepare himself for her. He was so shocked to see her and a baby that he didn't have time to warn his wife before the doorbell rang.

"I swear you need to turn that hearing aid up or get a new battery one. You don't hear me talking to you—" Gladys began as she came around the corner from the kitchen. The rest of her sentence had gotten stuck in her throat the moment she saw Natalia standing in her house.

No one said a word for what seemed like forever until Cecil cleared his throat and spoke.

"Ahem, let's go sit down so we can talk and get the baby fed. He looks like he is about to start fussing like your grandmother when she hasn't been fed," he joked, trying to lighten the mood.

It wasn't until that moment that Gladys noticed the baby carrier in her husband's hand and sucked her teeth. Not at the baby, but because his mama was so selfish.

"Really, Natalia? Lord, come on and take me now 'cause this child done lost the little bit of sense she had," Gladys said, walking right past her and into the other room.

"Come on boot, let's not start off on the wrong foot," he said. If his wife didn't calm down, he knew she was capable of letting anything come out of her mouth. He had told her so many times to think before she spoke, but to this day that has yet to happen. If it came up, it came out of her, and if you didn't like it she didn't care.

"The wrong foot started long before now, but I know one thing, if she don't hurry up out of my house, the right foot is going to be dead in her hind parts," she said with an attitude.

Gladys was a little old thing. She couldn't have been taller than four feet even, with hair the same color as her husband's that fell right to the bottom of her back. She had her Dominican roots to thank for that. Her skin was wrinkle free and her dark eyes always seemed to sparkle.

"Just hush up, Gladys! Let's hear what the child has to say."

"You know what, Poppa, don't worry about it. It was a mistake coming here," Natalia jumped in and tried removing her son from his hands. Cecil may have been small but he was still strong, as he continued to hold the carrier.

"Go sit down, Natalia," he simply said in a voice that she was all too familiar with. Whenever he spoke to her in that tone, she knew that he meant business so she obliged.

Walking over to the black leather loveseat, she sat down. Every movement she made, Gladys was clocking, waiting on her to say or do the wrong thing. Part of her hated that she had even come there, but the other part knew that she needed them no matter how upset they were with her.

Gladys stared a hole into the side of Natalia's face, but the shame she felt wouldn't allow her to look up, so she focused on getting a bottle ready. Her grandmother would always tell her that when people knew they were guilty of something they could never look you in the face. Especially if they did you wrong. That was the main reason that people

54

felt like they couldn't return to God when they stepped outside of His will. The shame of knowing that they did God wrong, not one time but multiple times, made them not cry out to Him.

"How have you been, baby girl?" he asked her, as she poured the formula into the bottle.

"She's back here. How do you think she's doing?" Gladys said sarcastically. Not bothering to address that statement, Cecil gave his wife a hard glare and turned back around to wait on Natalia to answer him.

"I've been ok."

"You sure?" he asked.

"I mean, yeah. I just really came to introduce you to your great grandson."

"Humph. Where is his daddy? Wait, let me guess, with his wife, perhaps?" Gladys said, reaching for the baby. Cecil was struggling, trying to get little Qy unbuckled and just like always, she was butting in.

"This is the last time I'm going to tell you to behave, woman," Cecil stated.

The moment she got the baby out of his seat, she cradled him in her arms and watched him closely. He was such a beautiful baby, but she knew he was going to have to deal with some challenging times in his life that his mother had caused because she was selfish.

"Give me that," she told Natalia reaching for the bottle she had just made him. As soon as she put it to his little lips, he latched on to it as if his life depended on it, causing Gladys to finally smile for the first time since Natalia had arrived.

"If you must know, Jaxon isn't with the alcoholic anymore," Natalia snapped, causing Gladys to finally make eye contact with her. If looks could kill, her grandfather would have been doing her eulogy at that very moment.

"The only reason I'm not going to slap the taste out of your mouth is because if you try and swing back, I'm going to jail. It's the 24th and my social security don't come until the third of the month, so I can't be bailed out. But come round here with that same nasty attitude that you got on the second, and see don't I feed you some of that gravel outside," Gladys said calmly.

Natalia knew she was serious because she had done it before. Had she not been so overwhelmed with her life right then, there would be no way that she would have even tried her grandma like that, but she knew it wasn't about to happen again.

"It is women like you that vex my spirit. You the side woman but have the nerve to get mad at the wife 'cause you sleeping with her man. How does that work?"

"If he was so much of her man then he wouldn't be with me every chance he gets," she retorted.

"Baby, let me tell you something. Just because a man has you in his bed does not mean he is choosing you over her. God won't send you anyone else's husband no way. Y'all newfangled women need to stop looking for Boaz 'cause honey, even that was Ruth's man. And you better believe when he found her, she was working not twerking! Now that piece of advice was free but the rest gone cost you," Gladys schooled her.

"Whatever," was all that she could think of to say. She knew her grandmother was right, but her pride wouldn't let her admit it and her heart wanted her to believe otherwise.

"Do you even know who the daddy is 'cause he shole don't look like that man."

Gladys may not have known Jaxon personally, but she was well aware of who he was and had seen him more times than she could count. From appearances on television or in magazines, he was everywhere, and the baby she was holding on to in her small arms looked nothing like that man.

"Of course I know who his father is!"

"If you say so, chile," Gladys said unconvinced as she waved her off.

"Baby girl, what's going on? We haven't seen you in a while," Cecil spoke. It pained him to see his grandchild so broken, but this was the life she chose for herself. On the outside, she looked well put together in her designer clothes, fancy hair, and luxury ride, but he saw past all of that. On the inside she was a mess, and he knew that she was there to have them to help fix her life, but he wasn't the one that could do it. She was going to need God Himself to work a miracle.

Many nights he had prayed for her and asked God what he needed to do to help her, but he couldn't touch the situation. Natalia more than likely would be upset when he told her his hands were tied, but he was going to follow God's commands.

"I just need a place to stay for a few days until I can get situated," she told him.

"And what happened to your apartment, Natalia?" he wanted to know. He could tell the way that she was shifting her eyes around the room she was about to come up with a lie, so he waited for it.

Natalia knew that if she told them that Jaxon was the one paying for her apartment this whole time and funding her account that they would be beyond upset with her. So she had to come up with something quick.

"Well, since I'm on maternity leave, I don't have money coming in like that right now," she said, hoping they would believe her but as soon as her grandmother opened her mouth, she knew that what she had just tried to sell them they weren't buying.

"In other words, Jaxon found out that wasn't his baby and so he stopped giving you money and put you out of the apartment he had you holed up in. The same apartment that

59

he told you he would leave his wife and big mansion for to come and be with you. Am I right, darling?" Gladys said reading her like a book. Natalia didn't know why she continued to try and get over on old Gladys because every time, she would bust her out in a lie.

"You don't have to tell me I'm right because the Lord has already shown me," Gladys continued as she handed the baby off to her husband. She had a feeling it was about to go down and she wanted to make sure that the baby was out of harm's way.

"Oh here we go with 'the Lord' showing you things again. Well did the Lord show you that I have AIDS? Did He? Since He shows everything else why didn't He show me how to prevent it? Your God is something else," Natalia screamed.

Before Cecil could put the baby down fast enough to catch his wife, she had already hauled off and slapped day into night from Natalia.

"Let me tell you something you little ungrateful bitty," Gladys started.

"Wait, let's just calm down for a second before this gets

out of hand," Cecil said calmly.

"No, Cecil! All of these years, she been walking around here giving us her tail to kiss and I'm tired of it. I listened to you long enough and now it's my time to talk."

Natalia knew that she had gone too far when she saw the tears falling from her grandmother's eyes, but she didn't care. She said what she meant. If God was so into showing people stuff, why didn't He show her what she needed to do and what not to do in order to prevent herself from living in this hell on earth.

"My God, as you call Him, is a mighty God!" she said through clenched teeth. "And had you been paying attention, He has showed you on more than one occasion that He was there for you, but you ignored him. It was Him that protected you from getting raped by numerous men that your mother had coming in and out of her life. It was Him that protected you the night that young boy Marcel and his friends held a gun to your head because my child owed them money for drugs she had stolen from them. It was my God that kept warning you in those dreams that you were having of your mother dying from that needle. Remember that? The same needle that she had contracted the same disease that you are carrying now. But no matter how much we loved on you and did our best to guide you and raise you, you didn't want it. And now you have the nerve to stand in my house and blame God? How dare you?"

"God doesn't care nothing about me! If He did He wouldn't allow my life to be like this," Natalia cried.

"God didn't do this Natalia, YOU DID! He gives us free will to make choices and you chose this life. Sleeping with men for money, carrying on relationships with married men, and now this," Gladys pointed to her son. "Bringing a baby into this world knowing that you have this deadly disease. How selfish can you be? Did you even try to prevent this from happening or did you only have this baby because of the financial freedom you thought he would bring?"

All Cecil could do was stand there and watch. Everything that his wife had just spoken on was nothing but the truth. He had to admit that he had a hand in this by not coming down as hard as he should have when Natalia was younger, but he honestly thought he could just love her through it.

"I didn't know that I had it when I got pregnant," Natalia said just above a whisper.

"Chile, that ain't no excuse. You out here rolling it around and dippin' low without protection?"

"But he didn't tell me he had it so how was I supposed to know?" Natalia cried, not moving Gladys one bit to making her feel sorry for her.

"Cecil, call the disciple that sits next to the Throne of God and tell him to let the Lord know I'm ready 'cause this chile done kilt me with her stupidity!"

"Nat, baby girl, it's no one's responsibility but your own to know your status. It's your body and we can't tell you what to do with it, but the least you can do is protect yourself, darling. Now you have this baby who will have to live the rest of his life this way, all because you were playing with fire," Cecil finally stepped in.

"It wasn't like Jaxon knew either. His wife was the one that told him. I'm sure if he had known he would have never put me in danger," Natalia said. Her grandparents may have thought she was trying to convince them that Jaxon was one of the good guys, but even with everything she knew about him, she was still trying to convince herself.

Before either one of them could speak again, Gladys

walked over to the phone on the wall and picked it up. Cecil thought she was just about to make another funny remark when the person she had called answered the phone.

"Shirley! Honey, I'm on the way, I got to get from out of this here house," she said before mumbling a few 'uh huh's' and hung up.

Both Cecil and Natalia watched as she walked to the front closet and grabbed her purse and her little Jitterbug phone off of the charger, and picked up the keys to their car from the table.

"Where are you going?" Cecil asked, knowing good and well she was not about to leave when they had this situation going on with their grandchild.

"Oh, I'm about to go get Shirley and we gonna meet up with Ruthie down to the Bango hall. You can stay here and minister to our grandchild since she seems to want to be babied. She can't take this meat I'm trying to feed her so you break out a bottle and a baby onesie for her tail and have fun. But I know one thing," she said turning her attention from her husband to Natalia, "if you leave this house, that baby better stay here. You won't be dragging my great grand out in these streets following behind a man that don't want you. That's what you not gone do!" And with that, Gladys turned on her heels and walked out the door.

"Jesus fix it," was all that Cecil could think of to say as he wrapped his arms around a crying and broken Natalia.

-7-

Focus was just something that Chey didn't have these days. Her world was torn apart by the one person that she had given her all to, and she didn't know how to move on. She felt stuck with no way out. Things had been so bad for her that she even stopped going to church on the regular, and only going if Von dragged her out. It was work and right back home for her. She was slacking and she knew it, but the motivation that she should have been finding in God felt like it could only be found in Qyree. But this was all her fault in the first place.

From the time she first met Qy, the attraction was there and part of her wanted something serious with him, especially after all of the time they spent together while in school. That time spent with him though, also let her know that he wasn't ready to be committed to anyone and she vowed to never let a man get her off her A game. The game was now over and she had lost. Chey began reminiscing on how everything played out.

Neither Chey nor Qy wanted to be at his parents' house any longer than they had been after the revelation that Zaria had revealed. To know that his mother was going to die all because her no good husband couldn't stay loyal was hard on him, and that meant that it was hard on Chey as well. The love that she had for Qy was like nothing she had ever experienced in a relationship, and she didn't want that feeling to go anywhere.

They made their way inside the hotel and headed up to their room. No words were spoken as Qy came out of his shoes and flopped down on her bed instead of going into his own room.

"Yo, what will I do without my mom?"

"Babe, she's still here so for now, just continue to do what you always have. Love her and support her through this. I know it's not easy but you're strong. And when you feel weak, that's what I'm here for," Chey smiled warmly, standing in front of him.

His eyes were closed and his breathing was choppy like he was trying his best to hold back the cry that wanted to escape his lips. He was biting down so hard on his lip that she knew he was about to draw blood soon.

Moving a little closer, she placed her hand on his leg. It was as if her touching him was the button that needed to be pushed for the tears to flow, and he lost it. Just her touch sent something to his brain that wasn't registering to him and he couldn't help himself.

"It's ok to let it out, Qy. Let these be your liquid prayers to God. He understands and He knows what's on your heart and mind."

Chey slid her sandals off and moved to the back of him and placed her arms around his stomach as he cried. He cried not just for himself, but more so for his mother. She didn't deserve this kind of pain and he wished he could take it away for her.

Feeling Chey hold him gave him some comfort, and he silently thanked God for her. She was his breath of fresh air and just what he needed at the moment.

"God, you knew this day would come even before we were created. And although we don't understand why all of this had to happen, we know that you will still get the glory out of this. Now Father, I ask you to help Qy know how to

68

deal with this and be able to move forward in you. Give this man of God the strength to not give up.

I pray for Zaria and everyone going through this, even Jaxon. Touch his heart and open his eyes to what he is doing so that he may be able to make a change in his life that glorifies you. And Lord, help me to be the constant unwavering support that my king on earth needs me to be for him. I know he will bounce back greater than he was before all of this, and I thank you and praise you in advance. In your son Jesus' name, I pray, Amen," Chey prayed.

As she opened her eyes, she looked right into the red eyes of her man. She had been so into her prayer that she hadn't noticed that he turned over and was now facing her. Qy brushed back a strand of her hair before telling her thank you.

Slowly, he moved a little closer to her face and touched her lips with his. Of course they had kissed plenty of times before, but this one was different. This one was so powerful that it felt as if their souls were connecting through their lips. It was undeniable that they had both just fallen in a love like no other.

In the back of Chey's mind, she knew what was about to happen but part of her didn't want to stop it. For all of these years, she had vowed to wait until she was married before she took that step, but right then she needed comfort and so did Qy. Was this the right way to go about it? Maybe not, but it was too late.

The warm tears fell from her eyes as she pulled away from their kiss. Sitting up, she repositioned herself so that she could begin removing her clothes as Qy touched her hands to stop her.

"What are you doing, Chey, baby?" he asked, searching her face for answers.

"Shhh," she told him and placed her index finger on his lips.

Returning back to her task at hand, she came out of her last article of clothing and walked over to her purse that sat on the footstool. Qy wanted to turn his head and tell her to put her clothes back on, but his mouth wouldn't cooperate and his eyes were connected to her body. It was perfect to him. She had just a little more weight on her than most of the women he used to date in his past, but not one of them could

70

hold a candle to her beauty.

He watched her as she slowly came back to him with a bottle of what looked like lotion in her hands, and then put it down on the bed. In front of him once again, she wiped the remaining tears he had on his face then lifted his shirt. She knew right then she had died and went on to glory, looking at him.

Qy on the other hand, was battling with what to do in this situation. The old Qyree wouldn't have tried to stop her, but he respected her mainly because she respected God and herself more. All of the other women didn't care so he was taught he shouldn't either. Chey was a different kind of woman and he cherished that.

"You don't have to do this, baby. I'm not pressed for it and I'm not going to get it from anyone else. I respect you too much and I understand how you feel about your body. You deserve a husband to share this moment with, not just a boyfriend," Qy did his best to reason. He realized that what he said made her even more willing when she pulled him to his feet.

Hearing Qy tell her how much he respected her and what

she stood for made her heart melt and her knees get weak, causing her to want this moment with him even more. The moment she had him fully undressed she wanted to run and hide. This was too much!

Instead of running like her mind was telling her to, she pulled the covers back and made him lay on his stomach. She sat beside him and poured some of the oil on to his back and began to give him a much needed massage. The tension in his body began to subside and it almost caused him to fall asleep, but he was afraid if he did he would miss something. The way she applied pressure to his neck and shoulders helped erase all of the events from the day and just focus on their now.

Finally, after she finished giving him one of the best massages he had ever received in his life, he turned his body over and pulled her to him. His hand moved up and down her arm while he looked into her eyes, searching for anything to let him know if he should stop. He found nothing. It was no turning back once he positioned himself, and she understood that. The moment their bodies connected, they were one. Not only in the natural but in the spiritual as well.

The next morning, Chey woke up in a state of bliss. Her

72

heart was genuinely happy but there was a small part of her that questioned her choice the night before. It felt so right to her, but there was that thought that God was a little disappointed in her actions no matter how beautiful it was, and she hated that. If there was one thing that she didn't want to do, it would be to disappoint God. But here she was feeling like what she had done was right in her eyes.

Falling asleep in his strong arms with their skin still touching was one of the best things she had ever experienced and she wanted to do it over and over again. As she thought back to how attentive he was to her, she couldn't help the smile that spread across her face as she looked to her left and noticed that Qy was no longer beside her. Immediately, she got up and headed to the bathroom before going to look for him.

Chey peeked out on to the balcony but he wasn't there, nor was he in the living room area. She saw his belongings still there so she knew that he wasn't gone, so he had to be in his room, but why? She opened the door a little and saw him on his knees in front of the bed with his head bowed in prayer. Not wanting to interrupt his moment with God, she backed up and went to go order them breakfast.

While she waited for both the food and Qy, Chey got dressed and did her hair. Today she would keep it simple and rock a pair of jeans, a fitted tee, and some sandals. Depending on what they were going to do for the day, her outfit was suitable.

"You ready?" Qy asked from the door, startling her. She looked up and smiled but the look on his face caused her to stop.

"I ordered us breakfast so we don't have to stop for a while, while we're out and about," she said, unable to read him. She watched as he let out a deep breath and tugged on his beard. He was stressed. It amazed her how in such a short time, she could pick up on things about him and vice versa.

"Nah, I'm good. We need to head out," he told her while walking away and not bothering to wait on her answer.

He began to get his things together as Chey watched him for a few moments before she followed suit. Something was off and she had hoped it had nothing to do with last night. The last thing she wanted was for him to look at her differently. Twenty minutes later, they had all of their things

74

and were pulling out of the parking lot with Chey not knowing their destination.

For a while as they drove, it was silence. Not the awkward kind but the one where they understood the other was in deep thought. For Chey, she was wondering if things between them would change for the better or if their one night of passion cost her something great. She was scared of the unknown but she wouldn't jump too far ahead. Qyree on the other hand had so many thoughts running through his mind at once.

The night he had shared with Chey was one he had never experienced before with a woman. The pure joy he felt being with her so intimately let him know that besides the chemistry they already had before they took that step was only enhanced once they crossed that line sexually. The oneness was unreal and he loved every moment of it. She was his forever but he needed to pull back.

What they had done could have possibly ruined her life and he wasn't for that. The last thing he wanted to do was hurt her but he had to let her go. It was for the best. When he had gotten up in the middle of the night, he watched her sleep for a while before he went to have a seat on the balcony. He thought about everything his parents were going through at the hands of his father, and got sick all over again. Not because of Jaxon, but because that was the first time it hit him that he could possibly be infected and if that was the case, he had just passed it on to the woman that he was deeply in love with. Being caught up in the moment, neither of them thought about protection because they hadn't planned on that happening. If it was anyone else, he would have been ready. As far as he knew, he had always strapped up with every female that he slept with, but the comment that Natalia made about the baby being his, made him wonder if she did something to the condom on one of the nights they were together. He had pulled back from her a long time ago, but there was still that possibility that she would have been that messy to do something like that. It was just the type of person she was.

Qyree had sat outside for almost four hours before he decided to go and get back in the bed. Walking past Chey, he watched as she breathed lightly while tangled in the sheets. Some of her body was exposed as he went over and covered her up some more. He was just about to get back in the bed and cuddle with her when his mind drifted to Natalia again and he froze. There was no way he could continue to be involved with Chey, so he made up in his mind he needed to let her go now. It was one of the hardest things he had ever had to do, although it would only be temporary. He very much still loved Chey and wanted a future with her, but he couldn't be the man she needed him to be right then. Although it was one of the hardest decisions he ever faced, he knew it was the only one he had right now. So instead of going back to bed with her, he went to his room and fell on his knees in prayer.

Turning his car around, he headed to the highway towards Valdosta.

"Where you going, bae?" Chey asked. She thought the reason he wanted to go ahead and go was to get their day started but it looked like they were heading towards home.

"Taking you home," he simply stated.

Confusion was evident on her face and without asking anything else, she just reached over and held his hand. He was going through it and she knew that he may just need his space for a while. The whole ride home felt faster than normal and before she knew it, they were pulling into her

77

driveway.

He got out and retrieved her bags and was about to get back in the car when she stopped him.

"What's going on, bae?" she questioned him. In her heart she knew something wasn't right and it scared her to death.

"I can't do this," he said pointing between the two of them. "It's not gonna work out like we want it to."

As soon as those words left his mouth the tears flowed. Not sad ones but the ones where you get so angry the only thing you can think of is to cry.

"Humph. All this time I thought you were changing but I guess the jokes on me, huh? As soon as I open my legs, that's it?"

"No baby, that's not it at all," Qy said trying to reach for her. Hitting his hand away and stepping back, he knew that she was hurt. The last thing he wanted her to feel like was he got what he wanted from her and then left her high and dry.

"Just go!" Chey yelled and ran into her house. He

78

wanted so bad to run after her and hold her in his arms and tell her to forget what he had just told her, but he couldn't. The fear of the unknown consumed him as he got into his car and drove off leaving the most important thing in his life behind him.

-8-

It was a dreary Saturday morning and it was looking like Von and Amir would be spending their day inside while the Lord had His way outside and let it rain. It didn't bother either of them one bit because they loved spending time together. The day that Amir decided he wanted to move with her, she was ecstatic, but part of her thought it may be a little awkward for the both of them considering their past. He wasn't used to her and she wasn't used to taking care of anyone but herself, but God had a way of working things out for the both of them.

"Mir, you want bacon or sausage with your waffles?" she asked him while she stood looking in the fridge for something to cook for them to eat. They had been up late last night watching movies, laughing, and eating popcorn, and got up a little later than normal but he still wanted breakfast.

"Bacon, please. Can I have cheese eggs too?" he responded from in front of the television as he played his game. He had waited all week to play because Von made it one of her rules that there was no gaming on school nights. Not once did he complain because he was used to that rule. His aunt and uncle, Nivea and Terrance, took school seriously and because of that he was a straight 'A' student.

"Boy, you eat like a grown man," Von laughed as she got all of the necessary ingredients and placed them on the counter before washing her hands and getting her pots ready.

"I gotta be strong so I can protect you, Mommy," he said, causing her heart to feel nothing but joy. Never had she imagined having this young man in her life would make her feel like this, but she thanked God for him every day.

Without another word, she got busy with her task at hand. She was just about to make the waffles and take the bacon out of the oven when Amir called out to her.

"Mommy, somebody is here," he yelled as he glanced out of the window with his controller still in his hand. He was hoping that his mother would come and see who it was so that he could get back to his NBA championship game on his PlayStation.

"Who is it?" she asked, wiping her hands and coming into the living room. She hadn't been expecting anyone and she knew for a fact that it wasn't grumpy pants Chey coming over. For the past few months, all her friend did was go to work and home so when she wanted to chill with her friend, she would pack up herself and Amir and invade her space for a few days.

Not too many people knew where she had moved to and she liked it that way, so whoever this was that was popping up unannounced at her home was about to get a piece of her mind. Peeking through the half opened blinds, the rain that was pouring down had whoever it was waiting for it to slow down before getting out. Looking around the couch where she was sitting earlier, she found her phone and dialed 911 without hitting send until she knew who it was that was at her home. The last thing she wanted to do was make a call that wasn't important, but the life that she previously lived still had her on edge.

Von stood there waiting as Amir went back to his game, losing all focus on who their guest was. She looked at the brand new Range Roger parked in her driveway and thought for a minute that it may just be someone visiting her neighbors because she didn't know anyone who drove a car like that. Just as the rain was letting up, the driver's side door opened and out stepped a tall built man. His face wasn't visible due to the hoodie he had thrown over his head to block out the rain that fell as he made his way to her front porch.

Surprisingly, there was something familiar about him and although she didn't know what it was, Von let her guard back down.

"Who is it mommy?"

"I'm going to go see now, baby. Just play your game," Von said, heading in the direction of her front door. With her phone still in hand and her thumb slightly over the green icon on her phone, she waited for her bell to ring.

"Who is it?" she yelled, looking to make sure that her locks were still in place and her alarm set. Von may not have been too alarmed but she wasn't crazy either. The last thing she wanted to do was cause any harm to come to her, or more importantly her son, so she remained on alert. That is until she heard the voice that answered her coming from the other side of her door.

"Tank."

It was at that moment she felt her knees get weak and her heart rate speed up. What was he doing at her house and better yet, how did he know where she lived? *Qyree*, she thought. That was the only explanation that she had as she put her phone down on the table beside the door and unlocked the door.

The minute he heard the locks being unlatched, Tank felt like his stomach had dropped to his feet and his heart was in his throat. Never had a woman made him feel this way before, ever. Not his first little school crush or even the woman he thought that he was going to marry while he was in the Navy, and especially none of the women that he dropped by to see with only one thing on his mind. After meeting Von a few weeks ago, he knew something was different and that's why it took him so long to come and holler at her.

When she opened the door, she had a look of shock on her face with a glimmer of appreciation that he was there. Dressed in a simple tank and pajama shorts with some long tube socks pulled up to her knees, her hair in a big poof ball on top of her head, and her face void of makeup, she was one of the most beautiful women he had ever seen in his life. Just looking at her and knowing her condition, he could tell she took very good care of herself.

"Hey," she started and stopped as she felt a presence beside her. Looking down to her left, Tank saw a little boy that could have been Von's twin staring back at him with a scowl on his face. On the inside he was laughing because he knew that this had to be her son, Amir, and from the looks of things, he played no games when it came to his mama.

"How you doing, sweetheart?" Tank said smiling at them both.

"She's fine," Amir said, never changing his demeanor.

"Uh, no sir, you will not be disrespectful to an adult," Von chastised, causing him to soften but only a bit. Amir was playing no games with Tank but that didn't bother him at all.

"Sorry, Mommy."

"It's all good, chief. I'm an only child, too, and the same way about my mama. I'm Tank," he said reaching his hand out to give Amir dap.

Quietly watching the exchange, Von stayed to the side to

85

see if Amir would respond with some manners this time around. When he reached out with a smile on his face to return the gesture, she let out the breath that she didn't know she was holding until that moment, just as a flash of lightening lit up the sky and a rumble of thunder sounded off, sending Amir running back into the house.

"Turn that TV off, Mir!" Von shouted behind him as she invited Tank in and closed the door. She was all good with him playing while it was just raining, but as soon as it sounded like the angels and disciples were in a bowling tournament in heaven, it was time to shut that all down. One thing that she had always remembered when she was at Nivea's grandparents' house was during storms they didn't play when it came to electronics being on when it was lightning and thundering outside.

"So what brings you this way?" she asked, walking back towards the kitchen.

Tank could smell the food she was cooking and instantly his stomach growled reminding him he hadn't eaten. He had gotten up that morning so nervous about popping up on Von that he had totally skipped out on breakfast which was something that he never did.

"Sounds like I need to be fixing you a plate, too," she giggled, causing him to blush.

"Only if you don't mind," he told her, taking off his hoodie and hanging it on the coat rack in the hall.

"Not at all. It's more than enough to share. Have a seat," she told him as she walked over to the stove and began fixing her son's plate first. Normally, she would make him eat at the table, but she decided to let him stay in the living room so that she could talk to Tank alone. If he had popped up out of the blue, he had to have something serious he needed to discuss.

"Mir, come and get your plate, baby," she yelled for him. Before she could even finish her sentence, he was bursting through the door with his hands out.

"Can I eat in my room, please?" he asked with wide eyes. Von looked at him amused that he was taking the presence of their guest to kind of get his way. He knew she didn't play about having food in any room other than the kitchen, but today he had hoped she would let him slide.

Peeping his game, she twisted up her lips before telling him, "Go ahead and you better not drop one piece of food."

Tank couldn't help but to laugh as he watched their interaction and thinking of his own mother and the relationship they had. He also admired Von, and looking around her home he could tell that she had a lot of the same taste that his mother had. It gave him such a welcoming feeling that he got lost in his thoughts. It wasn't until she set his food in front of him and spoke before he was pulled out of his thoughts.

"So Mr. Channing, what do I owe the pleasure of this visit?"

The way she said his first name made Tank want to do whatever he could possible to hear her say it every day for the rest of their lives. It was just that beautiful to his ears.

"Well," he began, "for starters, thanks for breakfast. It looks and smells wonderful. But I wanted to come and see what we could do about helping two of the most important people in our lives get back on track."

Before she could answer him, he bowed his head real quick while reaching for her hand and blessing their meal.

"Lord have mercy, he's a praying man," Von said to herself.

"My mama made sure of it," he said to her. Once again she realized that she had spoken out loud instead of in her head like she tried to. She was going to need to get a hold of herself when she was around him because there was no telling what she would be saying when he was near.

For a few minutes, neither of them spoke as they fed their faces. If Von couldn't do anything else, she knew she could cook. Another lesson she had learned from Mama Fran. Fran made sure to always teach the girls a new dish whenever they would spend the night at her house and they loved every moment of it.

The way the Belgium waffles with the strawberries, bananas, whipped cream, and homemade banana cream cheese melted in his mouth, Tank knew he was in love. If a woman couldn't do anything else for him, cooking was the way to his heart, and Von had just entered it and didn't even know it.

"Anyway, like I was saying, I can't stand to see my boy moping around like he's been doing," he said, grabbing both his plate as well as Von's and heading to the sink.

"I got it," she said, standing only for him to shake his

head and tell her to rest her pretty little feet. Another thing that drove him crazy were women with pretty feet. He was glad that she had socks on this day so he could concentrate, but he had already seen them the first time they had met.

Watching Tank take the initiative to help out with something so simple just drew her in to him even more.

"Do it Jesus," she started and stopped. The way her mouth kept betraying her by spilling her thoughts, she hoped that it hadn't done it again. Since he hadn't said anything yet, she knew that she was safe.

"So what's been going on with Qy?" Von asked as she watched him pull his sleeves up and submerge them in the dish water. Before he could reply, Amir came running in with his empty plate in his hand and the headset to his game on his head.

"Uh, sir, did I not tell you to turn that stuff off?"

"But Mommy, it stopped thundering and lightening," Amir said with pleading eyes.

Shaking her head, she watched as Tank reached out for his plate and even took a moment to find out what her son

90

was playing. Before she knew it, they were in a conversation about video games and Tank promising to take him on in a round or two of Mortal Kombat before he left. Von couldn't help but to smile at the interaction between the two while she straightened up and put the rest of the food away. For some reason, she imagined this being her life. A husband for her and a father for Amir. A loving relationship between them all and at the end of the day, being able to lay up in her man's strong chocolate arms, falling asleep, after planning their future together. But she knew in her condition that would never happen, so she did her best to stop entertaining the thought.

Once the two of them were done in the kitchen, they headed out to the living room and sat down on the couch. Since it was raining outside, the inside was a little chilly with the air on, so she reached and grabbed the throw that was on the back of the couch before tucking her legs under her and covering up her legs.

"You can take your shoes off if you want, unless your feet smell like Doritos," Von laughed, causing him to smile. She had jokes but he was the ultimate comedian.

Reaching down, he untied his sneakers and lifted one off

the floor.

"I don't know if they smell or not. You be the judge," he said as he shoved the shoe under her nose before she could get away. The harder she laughed and fought him off the more he wanted to be in her space. It took everything in him to pull back so that they could first talk about why he was there. Later he would tell her what else was on his heart.

It took Von a while to gather herself and to stop laughing. The way she was feeling, like she could just be her silly self around Tank, made her feel like she had known him all her life.

"Ok, so what's going on with my brother?" she asked, wiping the tears from her eyes.

By the way Tank's demeanor changed when she asked that, she knew it had to have been serious, and she would do anything to help get him out of his funk.

"As long as I have been in Qyree's life, I have never seen him like this and he is as close to a brother as I will ever get," he said sadly. Von could tell that this was also taking a toll on Tank as well, and she completely understood. It was the same way with Chey. She hadn't known her as long as

Tank had Qyree, but they couldn't have been any closer. When Chey hurt, so did Von and vice versa.

"One would think that he would be more upset about what went on with his father and his studio burning down, but all he talks about is Chey. Because they aren't on right now, he can't seem to focus on anything else."

Over the next hour, they both expressed what they knew from both Chey and Qy and did their best to come up with a game plan to get them back together. If not to immediately fix their relationship, then to at least talk things out and move forward. They now knew that neither of them wanted anyone else but the other, so at least that gave both Von and Tank hope that eventually things could work out. There was just one thing that Von had kept to herself that she knew wasn't her business to tell just yet. Hopefully it would come out when the time was right because if it came out before then, all hell would be breaking loose and there would be no hope of reconciliation between Chey and Qy.

"Can I ask you something?" Von said once they had been quiet in their own thoughts for a while.

"You can ask me whatever you like, doll," Tank said,

tugging on the blanket trying to get his arm under it. Von noticed that he had chill bumps on his arms as she slid a tad bit closer to him in order for the blanket to reach. Once they were comfortable again, she continued.

"When I told you what I was facing when we first met, why didn't you respond differently?" This had been something that she had wondered since their first meeting and had been on her mind ever since. His response was nothing like she had ever received from anyone other than Chey, and it threw her off. It was such a welcomed response that it had her thinking that maybe they could see each other more often, but part of her felt like it couldn't happen. She loved being a mother and making up for all of the lost time she had with her baby, but she was still a woman and she longed for a normal relationship with a man. Not that she needed one, but she had no trouble admitting that she wanted to be that Godly wife to someone one day.

It felt like she was waiting forever for a response from Tank, and she didn't know if what he was about to say was going to upset her and turn her away or not, so she just waited. The look on his face showed a little bit of embarrassment, but mostly uncertainty, so she placed her hand on his forearm to try and comfort him in some type of way. The initial thought she had, she knew she had to say a quick prayer of repentance 'cause that was not what God was telling her to do!

"When you told me about your status I wasn't appalled or anything. I actually admired you more because of how unashamed you were to let it be known. I'm not that confident yet," he explained and looked up into her eyes, waiting on a response.

Von's mouth opened to say something right before it snapped right back closed as the look of confusion that was on her face changed to one of revelation.

"You?" was all that she could get out. Instead of responding with words, Tank only nodded his head. For whatever reason, the embarrassment he immediately felt made him want to get up and leave, and he would have if Von hadn't stopped him.

"Please don't go," she said gently, reaching for his hand before he could stand up completely. The gentle and simple gesture gave him more comfort than he had felt in a long time, since finding out what he was living with. Blowing out a deep breath and looking into her beautiful brown eyes, he let God use this woman to help him become free of the bondage the enemy had him living in for so long.

-9-

"You do know this could cost us this paper, right?" Toni fussed at her son.

From the day that she found out she was pregnant by Jaxon, she knew that she had hit the jackpot. She would never forget the beat down that Zaria gave her when she caught the two of them that day. That was the first time that they had even slipped up like that, but the lust had gotten the best of them and they had to have it right then. That one decision could have cost her the life of her son that she was carrying.

After she left the house that day, she needed medical attention, so she drove herself to the hospital. Toni didn't dare tell them what really happened to her or who did it, so she lied and said she was robbed and didn't see the person. Once all of tests came back, that was when she found out that she was almost twelve weeks pregnant. When she calculated the time up, it was clear to her that the baby she was carrying didn't belong to Jaxon. Going on thirty years later, that was a secret not even her son knew and until she took her last breath, no one would ever find out.

The moment she told Jaxon she was pregnant he didn't ask any questions. He was actually happier than she had thought he would be and part of her just knew that he was going to leave Zaria for her. He had made promise after promise that they were going to be a family but by the time JJ turned three, she knew that wasn't going to happen. Right before she went to Zaria to let her know of their child together, he made sure to send a clear message to her that he would stop at nothing to keep her mouth closed.

Toni didn't care anything about all of that, she just wanted her man, and if she couldn't have Jaxon, then she would make sure that he came out of pocket for the child he thought was his. Now, here they were leaving the hospital from taking a paternity test for Natalia's baby, and she was scared out of her mind that somehow her secret would eventually be revealed. Until then, she would keep playing it cool like she always had.

"Man, who knew Natalia was the family bust down?" JJ asked her in a disgusted tone. He knew that she was sleeping with both his so called father and brother, but that only made it better for him.

Just like his mother. JJ was all about that mighty dollar. Anyway he could get it he wanted it, so when the opportunity presented itself that he could one day be head of the department that his dear brother wanted so bad, he jumped at the chance.

JJ didn't know a thing about the record company nor did he care to, as long as his pockets were fat and the women were plentiful. That way of thinking was what had him in the situation he was in.

As long as he could remember, his mother made sure she rubbed Qyree in his face. The pure fact that Qyree was living the life that he had always wanted made him even more determined to bring him down and take his place. Year after year, JJ yearned to have his daddy come be with him and his mother, but nothing would take him away from his family, leaving him and his mother to live with that void.

He watched his mother cry so many nights behind that man that he had even thought about taking Jaxon's life. Never finding a good enough way to get it done so that he wouldn't get caught, he decided to try something different.

The way Natalia talked about her feelings for Qyree, he was more determined to bring Qy down off of his pedestal, and getting her pregnant while taking the company right from under him would give him more satisfaction than ever. From the way that she would talk about him, he had thought the feelings were mutual between the two, not knowing that Qy couldn't care less about her. Little did he know that Qy also had his fair share of women just like Jaxon, and he didn't care a thing about any of them. Stepping to Natalia, he thought that he had finally won, and the dumb broad was just a clueless as he was. For him it was all about what he could use her for to get what he wanted out of them, but it was that way of thinking that had literally just cost him his life.

-10-

Chey sat on her bed and watched Von get ready for her date with Tank and smiled. She was so happy that Von was doing well in both her professional life as well as her personal. In the beginning, Chey had been a little worried that Von may fall back into her old way of thinking and return to jail like so many other women that she had known, but through prayer and hard work, she was a long way from where and who she used to be.

Von was being the best mother she could be to Amir and he adored her just the same, if not more. They were truly two peas in a pod and Chey thanked God that she was a part of their lives.

"You think this is too much?" Von asked, breaking Chey away from her thoughts. Von was wearing a cute royal blue romper set that showed off her curves, but not giving away too much. Her legs looked like God himself had sculpted them and the gold heels she wore only accentuated them more.

Chey had relaxed Von's hair and flat ironed it straight before braiding it into a neat halo braid circling her head. The gold jewelry and accessories went well with the look, and her makeup was natural but still popping. Her girl was fierce!

"Oh hush! Channing is going to love it," she waved her hand dismissing the negative thought that had come to Von's mind. She understood that this was her first real date and her friend was nervous. But she wasn't about to let her talk herself out of this night.

"You sure you are up to watching Mir tonight?"

"No ma'am, you are not about to play this game. You know my nephew is no problem at all," Chey told her.

"I'm not worried about him misbehaving, I'm just concerned if you are feeling up to it."

"Girl, yeah. That spell passed hours ago and I know it was because I hadn't eaten all day. I got behind at work and food was the last thing on my mind," she lied, as she got up and headed to the front of the house with Von hot on her heels.

If Chey wanted to play like Von was dumb, she would go right ahead and let her at that moment, but she would be sure to call her out on it later. Chey thought Von didn't know she had been still stressing about her relationship with Qy and it was causing her to almost stop caring for herself. For weeks after their breakup, Von had to literally drag Chey out of the bed to make sure she went to work, ate, and even showered. Lately she had been returning back to herself but she still had a long way to go. Von just prayed that it would be soon.

As worried as she was about Chey, Von was so excited to be going on a date. The feeling she had swelling inside of her stomach felt like there were bats fighting and she seriously needed them to get themselves under control before Tank arrived.

The day that he had come over to her house to talk with her about Chey and Qy and how to get them back together, was the day that she knew she had fallen for him. With him trying to help get things together with the music company and her managing being a mommy, student, and working full time, this was the first time they were both free to go out. The phone conversations and texts were fine, but they were so eager to have some time in person together. Since the next day was Saturday and they had planned to do something with Amir, Tank wanted this night to be just about them and she was ready.

"You look pretty, Mommy," Amir looked up and smiled at her once she walked into the room.

"Thank you, baby. Make sure you take care of your auntie, ok?" Von smiled.

"I will. She will be alright. I will be her protector until Uncle Qy comes back," he said, returning his attention back to his iPad. Not really understanding how that statement affected Chey, he didn't think twice about what he had said. All he knew was that his aunt missed his new uncle and she was sad because of him not being there. So until he came back, Amir would be the one to protect her.

A lone tear fell from Chey's eye and she quickly wiped it away. The last thing she wanted was for Amir to think he had said something wrong when that wasn't the case. Just as Von was about to pick up her phone to call and get a rain check for dinner, the doorbell rang.

"Saved by the bell," Chey said while giving her best attempt at a smile as she walked to the door.

Well dang! Chey thought to herself once she opened the door and saw Tank standing there. If he didn't make a nun want to leave the monastery and make a blind woman pray that she could see, she didn't know who could. Unless it was her boo, of course. No one in her opinion could ever take his place in the looks department, but Tank was surely coming in as runner up. She guessed it was something about those Reeves men DNA that was in their blood.

Standing before her in a white button up with the top two buttons open, a burgundy blazer, some khaki pants that looked like they were sewn onto his body, and some burgundy loafers, Tank was impeccable. His hair was freshly cut and the lineup of his facial hair was too clean. The simple watch and lone necklace with the cross on it hung loosely around his strong neck, finishing out his look.

"Hey, you must be Channing. It's nice to finally meet you," she smiled once she finished giving him the once over.

"And you must, Cheynese. I was worried for a second that I may be at the wrong house 'cause your face was unreadable," he laughed as he went in for a hug.

And he smells good! Von better lock him down like

yesterday!

"I'm sorry about that, my mind is just all over the place these days," she told him as she moved out of the way so that he could come in.

Shutting the door behind him, she moved around him to lead him into the front room where his date should have been waiting, but she was nowhere to be found.

"Tank!" Amir shouted and jumped up from his seat on the floor, full speed ahead to where Tank stood.

"My main man," Tank replied, genuinely happy to see Amir as well. This may have been the first time Chey had officially met Tank, but she could see nothing but adoration in both of their eyes as they caught up on 'guy stuff' as Amir called it.

Before she had a chance to go searching for Von, she appeared from the back with her purse. The look of approval was evident on Von and Tank's faces as they took in the appearance of one another. The way he looked at Von was the same way that Qy would always look at her, and she missed that something terrible. The way Qy's eyes would sparkle with a smile and his lips would curl into this cute

106

little position whenever she was around him, always made her feel like she was the most beautiful girl in the world.

Instead of dwelling on those thoughts that were sure to have her holed up in her bed not wanting to face the world, she threw those thoughts aside and ushered the two love birds out for a night of fun, and hopefully the beginning of a beautiful romance. Someone deserved to be happy and in love, and she couldn't think of two people who should experience it more than them.

"Go have fun you two, and bring me dessert from wherever you go for dinner," she laughed, walking them to the door.

"Anything for you, sis," Von said as Tank took her hand and walked her to the car. Once again closing the front door and locking it, Chey went back to where Amir was.

"Netflix and chill, auntie?" he asked her.

"Boy, what you know about some Netflix and chill?" she laughed as the two of them went into the kitchen to find every unhealthy food she could think of for them to stuff their faces with. If she couldn't be with the man that she loved, she definitely didn't mind being with the boy that had managed to steal her heart as well.

-11-

The smooth sounds of Babyface flowed through the speakers in the car as Tank maneuvered the car down the street. Von was so relaxed and at ease with Tank and she had only been in his presence a little while, but it felt like forever. Their chemistry was crazy and she prayed that he was heaven sent just for her.

"What you know about this song?" Von smiled. "Soon As I Get Home" was one of her favorite Babyface songs. All of the things he talked about doing for his woman was something she had always dreamed that someone would do for her. But the way her life had been set up, she had lost all hope. Until now.

"What you mean? Babyface is that guy! He knew exactly what to say to set the mood. I was probably conceived during one of his songs," Tank laughed. The deepness of his laughter did something to Von. It was so smooth yet rough, calming but it made her nervous. She had never heard anything so sweet before in her life and all she wanted to do was hear it forever.

Wayment Von, don't get carried away. Technically, this is only date number one and you trying to marry the man again just like when you met him the first time, she chastised herself in her head.

"You trying to be wifey already?" Tank asked. Von was mortified. She had to stop doing that.

Although she was embarrassed yet again about speaking what should have been her secret thoughts, she still had to lay something out for him.

"Oh no baby, I'm not *wifey* material. I'm cut from a different cloth. See a *wifey* is someone who will never be a wife. That's just a term that a lil' boy gives to his so called girl to make her feel important. He feels like if he pacifies her with that position she will be content in that spot. She feels like she has the upper hand on every other woman that catches her man's eye when no other woman should catch his eye because he ain't throwing it at them. Feel me? I used to think that being called wifey was cute but life has a way of opening our eyes.

Now a *wife* is a woman who her man cherishes enough to

110

give her his last name. He knows she is worthy of the crown that she wears as his queen. Not only does he know her worth and embraces it, but she knows her worth and won't settle for less," she broke down her logic for him.

Glancing over at her and then back at the road, he thought about everything she had just said. Deciding not to say anything right away, he just nodded his head and turned the music back up. Von didn't know if she had turned him off or not, but she really didn't care. She knew who she was and how valuable she was to God, and the man that came into her and her son's lives had to value her as well. If what she said had offended him, oh well; it was what it was and she was standing firm on it.

Von looked out the window and could feel herself getting an attitude. Her flesh was telling her to curse him out and take her back home so she could get her son, and to lose her number. She couldn't though, because it felt like God was pinching her lips shut so tight she knew if she looked in a mirror she could see His fingerprints.

She was so deep into her feelings she hadn't even realized that they had come to a stop in front of a restaurant until she felt her door being opened.

"Good evening, madam," the man whom she assumed was the valet attendant greeted her as he held his hand out for hers. Slowly, she placed her hand in his and allowed him to help her out of the car as Tank came around to meet her. Looking at him, she couldn't read what he was feeling and once again, God covered her mouth to prevent her from sucking her teeth. Before He could place His other hand over her eyes, she rolled them as hard as she could, causing Tank to chuckle slightly.

"You so petty," he said, leading the way to the door after handing over his keys. It was quiet for a Friday night, Von thought, before they made their way into 306 North, which was a classy based restaurant, let some tell it, so she was surprised that it was empty on a Friday.

"Good evening, Mr. and Mrs. Reeves. Everything is ready, please follow me," the hostess said. This time God held her eyes from rolling. Her being called 'Mrs. Reeves' didn't go unnoticed and before their little episode in the car, it may have flattered her but right then, it didn't. She couldn't figure out why she had such a big attitude all because Tank didn't respond to what she said in the car, but the moment she laid eyes on the sight before her all of that

112

attitude she had instantly vanished.

Tank had rented out the whole place just for the two of them. There were rose petals decorating the floor in her favorite color of royal blue. Never in her life had she seen flowers that color so she knew they had to have been special ordered just for her. The table was set beautifully with candles lit and the staff was beside their table waiting for them.

"Oh my God, this is beautiful," Von spoke with her voice cracking. No one had ever done anything like this for her and truth be told, she probably wouldn't have appreciated it back then if someone had tried.

"I didn't respond to what you said in the car, not because I was offended or anything. I was quiet because you opened my eyes to something I had never thought about. I understand where you're coming from not wanting to be labeled as my wifey, and I respect you more for opening up to me and letting me know how you should be treated. So if you would let me, I would love to show you how my woman, my love, my better half, my supporter, and one day my *wife* should be treated," Tank told her, taking her breath away.

I know that justice of the peace gotta have an after-hours number or something!

The way Tank's eyes smiled as he laughed that laugh Von loved so much, she knew that once again her mouth had betrayed her. But this time she didn't care as she brought his smile to an abrupt end as she let her lips meet his.

-12-

"Sometimes we have to step away from formalities during service and get a little selfish with God. Life and its many obstacles make us have to cry out because a silent prayer just won't do. And although there are others going through just like you are, you need this for you. You know that your life depends on that very moment and if you miss crying out to Him for yourself, there may not be another opportunity," Chey stood behind the mic looking out into the congregation. It had been so long since she was in God's face and she needed him more than ever. If He didn't fix her life and situation, she didn't know how she was going to make it. Shame and depression seemed to be consuming her and she felt herself on the verge of giving up.

"Made a way. Don't know how but you did it. Made a way. Standing here not knowing how I'll get through this test," she began singing making Travis Greene's "Made a Way" personal for her. This song had been on repeat for the last few days and she knew that the only way she was able to stand and sing that song was because of her faith in God to make the impossible possible.

"You move mountains. You cause walls to fall. With your power. Perform miracles," she continued. "No matter how big your issue is and how small you may feel, you have to trust God, church. Sing, you made a way, don't know how but He did it. I don't know why but I'm grateful."

Chey couldn't stop the tears from falling no matter how hard she tried. With her hands raised, all she could do was cry out in her heavenly language as the praise team finished the song for her. The tempo slowed down as she gathered herself enough to open her mouth again.

"I'm standing here only because you made a way," she barely whispered. "You moved mountains you caused walls to fall! You caused chains to break. Hey! And giants fall, hey, 'cause you moved mountains. Mountains are moving church! Strongholds are breaking church! Glory to God! When the doctors said no Mother Ann, God said yes!" she pointed to one of the mothers of the church that had been diagnosed with cancer but was now in remission.

There was no one in that building that was able to control

116

their praise. People were kneeling at the altar or in front of their seats. Faces were full of tears as they cried out to their God while He made His presence known throughout the room. There was no denying the presence and power of God at that moment and that was exactly what Chey needed. She had absolutely no strength on her own but right then, she was reminded that she didn't need to rely on her strength because she had God's working on her behalf.

As soon as church was over, the first thing Chey wanted to do was get something to eat and head home to lay down. She had a busy schedule the next day since it was the beginning of the work week, so she wanted to make sure she got enough rest. Her body was screaming for her to take a break and today she was about to obey.

"Where you rushing off to so fast, young lady?" Chey heard her mother ask. Francine Broadus wasn't her biological mother but was her maternal grandmother. After the passing of her parents, Francine and her husband Davis took on the role without a second thought. Chey was their only grandchild and they loved her more than anything. There would be no way that she would end up in the system and if they had to, they were going to fight tooth and nail to get her. Luckily they didn't have to go through the courts because of the seriousness of the situation, and they were well known in their community so it made the process a smooth one for them all. Chey owed everything to them and there wasn't anything she wouldn't do for them.

"I'm hungry and need some rest. Tomorrow is going to be a long one," she replied, looking into her mother's beautiful toffee colored face. Her silver, almost white, hair was freshly pressed and pulled into an elegant ponytail to the side of her head. The bright yellow hat that she wore matched the shirt that was underneath her white pant suit and the yellow and white sling backs she wore on her feet were to die for. To be a little old lady, Francine always slayed when she stepped out the door.

"Well, you make sure you call me tomorrow afternoon and let me know how you are feeling. If I don't hear from you by supper time, please know I will be knocking on your door," Francine sassed. Chey knew she was dead serious too, and she wanted no parts of that fussing out she would be sure to receive.

Before she could respond and let her know she would definitely be getting a call, they were rudely interrupted.

"So you take my man and then turn around and act like you don't owe me an apology?" Chey and Francine heard from behind them. Turning around to face the voice, they looked right into the vindictive eyes of none other than her former best friend, Natalia.

Neither of them had seen one another since the incident at Zaria's house and because of how Chey was feeling about the whole thing, if she never saw Natalia again in life, it would still be too soon. A few days after everything jumped off, Natalia did make attempts to call Chey. Not because she was worried or sorry for her, but because she wanted to fish for information as well as rub things in her face. Chey was so distraught over the status of her relationship with Qy, she never answered or returned the calls.

She had plans on calling Natalia once she got her mind together, considering they had been friends all this time, but when Natalia got beside herself and started leaving nasty voicemails and texting her all kinds of nonsense, Chey said forget it. That's when it finally hit Chey that Natalia wasn't her friend for real, and this face to face further proved her point.

The moment Chey turned to face Natalia, she could tell

119

that Chey had been going through it and that little piece of revelation caused a sly smirk to spread across her face. Natalia had always been jealous of Chey because she seemed to have everything she wanted. For some reason, the fact that they were both being raised by their grandparents, their real parents were dead, and they both had pretty good childhoods didn't matter one bit to Natalia. In her eyes, Chey was everyone's favorite. But she couldn't lie and say she didn't once care for Chey or consider them friends. They were absolutely friends all the way up until the fifth grade when boys started being interested in Chey and not her. It didn't take much for her heart to become bitter and to this day, she was still bitter.

"Ok, let's be clear. For one, I owe you nothing and two, Qyree was never your man. Just because you tooted it up and threw it back does not mean y'all were in a relationship," Chey went off. She knew now may not have been the perfect time or place to have this discussion and she would do her best to not get disrespectful in the Lord's house, but she was way over the capacity of being able to deal with the devil and his minions.

"You ain't no better than me!" Natalia got loud, causing

the few members that were still lingering around to look in their direction, including Von. It was about to go down.

"No ma'am, we are not doing this in here," Von said, walking over to where the three women were. Not too far behind her was Tank and Amir. Tank looked down at Amir and told him to go and wait outside. If the women got to fighting, he didn't want Von's son to see her in that way. Amir hesitated a few seconds but thought it would be best to follow the directions he was given.

"Who you supposed to be?" Natalia looked at her disgusted. This was the first time she had ever seen Von, but there was something vaguely familiar to her. She just couldn't put her finger on it.

"Don't worry who I am. I know you. All you need to worry about is moving around and making your way up out of here. My sis may not be bout that life but I *just* put my shoes on for this Christian walk and don't mind putting one clean through your back," Von voiced as she took her earrings off, moving closer to Natalia. Before she could get any closer, it was like a light bulb went off in Natalia's head.

"Ohhh, I know where I know you from! You up here

calling somebody 'sis' and acting like you deserve the friend of the year award, but aren't you the girl who had her best friend set up to be raped a few years ago?"

The sickness that washed over Von was apparent on her face. It had been all over the news in Georgia at the time, and the media did not go easy on her and she understood now that they should have because she deserved it. But she had changed, repented, and apologized more times than she could count. The relationship between her and Nivea had been really good and she had been forgiven, but there were still some days where it was hard for her to get past what she had done to her friend.

"That was a real low blow, Natalia, but I guess since all you know how to do is give *low blows,* that should be expected," Chey said, catching everyone off guard. Francine knew that she needed to stop this but the words that she sought were nowhere to be found. The look on Natalia's face was priceless, but she still was doing her best to hold her ground. She had to admit that stung more than she wanted to let on.

Besides the tired look in Chey's eyes, she was still flawless as Natalia used her own eyes to roam over Chey's body and take in her appearance.

"Sweetie, please get down off of that high horse that you have always been on. You're no different than me. Only good for one thing and Qy made sure to fill me in and up a few weeks ago," she spat while she took her hand and patted right below her navel.

"See, you've gone too far now," Francine finally found her words as Tank caught Von in midair when she lunged for Natalia's throat, barely missing her.

"The next time you cross paths with my daughter, coming at her like you crazy, especially in the Lord's house, please believe it's gonna take Jesus and all twelve of his disciples to get me off your butt. I may be old but I will still get down about mine. Now walk out before you get drug out," Francine said through gritted teeth.

Natalia may have acted crazy, but she was far from stupid and knew that Mrs. Francine was not playing games with her. Giving both Von and Chey one last look, she marched towards the back of the church and saved herself from that beat down.

"Babyyyy, Mama Francine got that Judas spirit. I just

knew she was about to cut that girl's ear off," Von said

hyped up. Everyone turned in her direction and looked at her

to see if she was serious about what had just come out of her

mouth.

Seeing the confused look on her face, none of them could

stop the laughter from escaping their mouths as she looked

on trying to figure out what was so funny.

"Von, darling, I will see you this week at bible study

'cause you need just a tad bit more tutoring," Francine

laughed as she kissed Chey, Von, and Tank's cheeks before

walking off in search of her husband. It was date night and

she was more than ready.

"What's so funny?" Von asked, still not getting the joke.

"Sis, Judas didn't cut anybody's ear off, it was Peter who

did it," Chey explained with the best straight face she could

give. Her insides were about to burst from holding in the

laugh that wanted so bad to come out, but instead of causing

further embarrassment, Chey gave them both a hug before

leaving.

"I'll see you in the morning at eight, right?" Chey asked

before getting in her car after they made it outside.

"Yup, right after I drop baby boy off at school," Von told her. As if Amir had some type of device on that caused him to know when his name was mentioned, he popped up from the small playground, ready to go.

"Bye, auntie," he said, throwing his arms around Chey's waist and laid his head on her stomach, squeezing as tight as he could.

"See you later, TeeTee's man." Placing a kiss on his chocolate forehead, Chey said her final goodbyes and drove off. She was hungry and if it was ever possible, she could have sworn her stomach was touching her back. Food was the mission and she was about to conquer it.

-13-

Qyree looked down at his phone for what seemed like the millionth time and just like before, he couldn't bring himself to hit the green phone button and place that much needed call. It had been almost five months since he seen or spoken to Chey, and as much as he wanted to hear her sweet voice, he just couldn't bring himself to do it. He knew he was wrong for the way he ended things, but he felt like being out of her life would be better for her. It was something his mind thought but his heart was not in agreement. It craved her.

"Baby, you need to call her," he heard his mother say softly behind him.

Turning his head, he was met with the tired eyes of his mother from her hospital bed. Zaria had been hooked up to all of these machines and cords for the last week, and she seemed to be going downhill at a rapid pace, which broke him down even more. It was as if once she had revealed her secret, she just stopped taking care of herself. He wondered if she was only taking care of herself long enough to decide on when she wanted to let him know and once she did, she stopped.

"It's better if I don't, Ma. She's better off," Qy sighed, tugging on his beard. As frustrated as he was, it wouldn't be long before he had pulled every strand from his face.

"How is she better off? The man that she fell in love with who claimed he loved her decides to leave her the morning after she gave him something so precious?"

Qyree looked on in shock as to how his mother knew when he left Chey. He had waited a short time after to tell her they were no longer together and even then, it wasn't by choice. Zaria knew that something was up when she stopped hearing Chey's name on the regular, so she asked her son about her whereabouts. All he told her was that they had decided to cool it for a while and left it at that. So hearing that his mother knew what really happened let him know that this bit of news could have only come from one person, Cheynese.

"Trust me, Ma, I didn't want to leave her. Especially right after something so important. I mean, that's something that I would do to those other broads but not her. She was different," he told her, standing up and moving closer to her side of the bed.

Zaria had lost so much weight and her skin didn't hold the same vibrant look that he had seen his whole life. This illness was breaking her down so fast and they both knew that the doctors had no hope that she would walk out of there alive. So they made sure to keep her as comfortable as possible until that time came. Qy on the other hand had been reintroduced to a powerful God and all of his faith was in Him.

"If she was so different as you say, then why did you treat her like those other women?" Zaria asked before going into a fit of uncontrollable coughing. Qy tried to help her sit up and drink some water from her cup, but she waved him off while pushing the cup out of her face gently. That one simple movement alone felt like she had tried to move a car by herself rather than a cup. Her body was so weak and she knew that it would only be a matter of time before it gave out completely on her. Although she was tired, she knew that there was only one thing that needed to happen before she would be okay with her fate, and that was to have her son reconcile with the only woman she felt like would take care of her baby. She could literally rest in peace knowing that Qy had someone who was good for him, to be there for him, 'cause his no good daddy wasn't going to do it. *Ole bastard*, she thought.

Once the coughing ceased, Qy answered her.

"I didn't treat her like them," he said with a confused look on his face. How could anyone say that he had treated her like those other loose women when he had completely changed his ways because of her? Not once in his life had he ever courted a woman, been faithful, put her needs before his, let her lead him back to God, or respect her body like he had done with Chey.

"So you never had sex with a woman and then left her, severing all ties?"

"Well yeah, but this wasn't like that," he tried to validate his point, but he really didn't have one.

"Hmm, really? So after she let her wall down with you, trusted you, and gave you something that she cherished so much because she thought you valued her, did you not leave her the very next day and it's been months since you reached out to her?" she asked. When Zaria put it that way, immediately he understood what she meant and he felt like the scum of the earth.

"I didn't mean to hurt her, Ma, I promise. It's just that with everything that happened with Jaxon, the company, and then your situation, I couldn't think straight. I felt like I wasn't going to do anything but hurt her more so I had to let her go. She deserves better than me," he stated. Plopping down in the chair, he covered his head with his hands and looked down to the floor.

"Baby, listen," Zaria began. "The things that transpired had to so that all of our eyes could be opened. We all have been so blinded to the truth and God had to shake up our lives in order for us to wake up. Do I wish things had played out differently? Absolutely, but our way of thinking and the way we would handle situations are nothing like the ways of God. He has His own reasons for what He does and contrary to the way things may look, His ways are perfect. I believe in my heart that Chey was brought back into our lives at the appointed time. God presented her to you all of those years ago so that you would know what He had waiting for you, but it wasn't time for the two of you. You had to grow some more, you had to go through some things in order to appreciate her when she came back around."

Qyree sat and thought about what his mother was saying and it was so clear to him when she put it the way she had. The moment he had set eyes on her, there was something about her that drew him in but not too far. She was guarded and needed someone that was going to prove to her that he would take care of her heart. That wasn't him back then because his way of thinking was only on one thing. Had he started something with her in college, he was sure to break her heart into nothing but dust, and now he felt like he still ended up doing that same thing.

"It's my fault that you turned out like Jaxon. Had I been strong enough in myself and in God, then I would have walked away a long time ago, taking you with me. All you knew was how he treated women and that your mother was aware and did nothing. The arguing and fussing that we did on the regular was not me taking action the proper way. He was only doing what I allowed him to do to me and you witnessed that. No child should ever have to experience the things you did and I wish mothers would think about those things before or even during relationships with these men. A woman can grow up thinking that the way her mother is treated is the way she should be, and a boy will think that's how he should treat his women. They may not say anything but their actions in life will be the clear indicator.

Son, change your way of thinking. Do you want your own kids to one day feel all of the pain that you are feeling in this moment, or do you want to be the one to set a new standard? You don't have to be like Jaxon because look where that has gotten him," she finished right as the door to her room opened. He had a lot to think about and more importantly pray about.

"Don't be looking at him like that, Brittanie. He's engaged and a one-woman man," he heard Zaria say to her young nurse. From the look on Brittanie's flushed red face, he could tell she was embarrassed but he also thought about the fact that he hadn't paid her any attention when she walked in the room.

Qyree was never the one to miss out on an opportunity when he crossed paths with a woman, especially if she was feeling him from the jump. Just that small revelation in that moment let him know that he was changing and he needed to go and make things right. He had waited long enough and it was time to get his queen back, but would she still be

132

Heaven Between Her Thighs
Denora Boone

available?

-14-

Hitting the locks on his car, Qyree got inside with his parents' house on his mind. He had been at the hospital for the last two days with his mother, so he was in need of a change of clothes and a good shower. While he was there, he was going to get a few things for her so that he could do his best to get her to feeling like her old self. If that meant bringing her one of her designer night gowns and all of her beauty essentials, then that was what he was going to do.

Everything that his mother had talked to him about was weighing heavy on his heart, and all he could think about was seeing Chey, wrapping her in his arms, and apologizing over and over until she took him back. Once again, she had opened his eyes to the things he hadn't even thought about. But that spirit of fear caused him to continue in the direction he was going in.

Hearing his phone go off in the cup holder beside him, he hit the Bluetooth button on his steering wheel and glanced at the screen on the dashboard once it connected. Jaxon had been blowing his phone up recently and he knew that it was only because Qyree found out he had something to do with the burning down of his studio and the police were asking questions. Jaxon probably wanted to find out what they were saying to Qyree, or better yet what Qy was saying to them. Just like the many times before, he sent him right to voicemail at the same time another call was coming in. This time he answered.

"What's good bro? You all booed up now and don't holla at ya boy no more," Qy laughed. It felt good to be able to smile or laugh, considering that he hadn't done much of either lately.

"You got jokes, huh? You know what it is," Tank replied, with a smile a mile wide spreading across his face. He couldn't even argue with Qyree about him being booed up because he was. Ever since he had been kicking it with Von, it was like his whole world had changed and it was a welcomed one.

"Yea, I know. Sis got my boy whipped."

"I do not!" he heard Von yell in the background as she giggled.

"See, she couldn't even say that with a straight face," Qy said. Tank and Von may have spent a lot of time together but he made sure to check in on his boy on the regular so Tank knew that Qy was just messing with him.

"What you got going on?" Tank asked.

"Bout to head to the house and get myself a shower and some clean clothes. I been at the hospital and need to wash that off of me.

It sounded like Tank was moving around, before he heard a door close and the background noise become a little quieter before his cousin spoke again.

"How Auntie doing?"

"The same, man. I hate seeing her like that and it messes me up to know there is nothing that I can do to help her."

"Yeah, it's tough, but we gotta be there for her no matter what," Tank told him, trying his best to sound optimistic. He hated to be reminded of what his aunt was going through, knowing that one day he too would face a similar fate. He just planned on taking care of himself the best way that he could to extend his time here with the ones he loved. As much as he understood Zaria and the decision she made, he just couldn't bring himself to let himself go. Especially now that he had Von and Amir in his life. They were his new reasons to keep pushing and fighting.

"Yeah, you right. What you and sis got going on today?" Qy said changing the subject. He wasn't in the mood to talk about his mother's condition at that moment. He needed to just breathe for a few.

"Just left church with the fam and picked up something to eat."

"I gotta get my mind together so I can come to church. I know I been missing out and I hate that."

"Well it was good that you didn't come today 'cause there was a visitor 'bout to get the right hand of fellowship," Tank said sounding amused.

"And the left too!" Von yelled out.

"Girl, gone and quit actin' up," Tank laughed. It sounded like a door shutting again and Tank paused before smacking his lips like he had just drunk something.

"Peep this though, Natalia came to church today," Tank

paused. He knew Qy was about to go off any moment.

"For what?! Did she light up in flames? You know demons can't be in the house of God too long," he said seriously, causing Tank to sound like he was choking.

"For real, I was waiting too. But nah, she called herself confronting Chey and you know my bae is wild. I had to hold her back from laying ole girl out. She was coming out her earrings and everything. Then Mrs. Francine almost let her inner 1970's Foxy Brown out. I promise God was going to have to call me home if Mrs. Francine got to fighting that girl. Can you imagine all of the mothers from the mother board goin' at it with her?" That visual alone had both Tank and Qy with tears in their eyes. Leave it up to his cousin to be stupid and get him out of his funk, even if it was for a little while.

"So Chey good?"

"Yeah, sis straight. You can tell she's hurt and Natalia saying that you were with her a few weeks ago didn't help."

"She told her that? Man, that girl lying," Qy said in his defense.

"Trust, I know. I don't think she really believed her or anything, but it was just a shock, know what I mean?"

"I hope so."

"But look, this what I called you for," Tank said, quickly getting to the nature of his call. He had been outside too long and he knew that Von would be coming to check on him in a minute. He needed to get this out before she did.

"What's up?" Qy asked sensing the seriousness in his voice.

"Do you think it's too soon for me and Von to take that next step?"

Qy could tell that Tank was holding his breath waiting on his answer. It had only been a few months since they had been kicking it but from the looks of it, things were getting serious. The way the two of them took care of one another on so many different levels, was remarkable, and Von's son, Amir, was right there with them. Von had been worried about getting involved with Tank in the beginning, but it was her son that pushed the two of them together. Amir was so happy to have Tank in their lives and it mattered to him that his mother was happy too. It made him think about what his mother had just told him in the hospital and this was a prime example.

"On the real cuz, love has no time limit on how fast it happens. If you've prayed about it and your heart is telling you to do it, then you have my support. That's sis anyway and I know she's good for you. Shoot, she turned me down before I even said anything to her, so I know she not on no games," Qy laughed, thinking about the time they met.

"You tried to holla?"

"Well, not exactly. I only saw her and Chey from behind when I first saw them that day. When I finally got their attention, her face was already tooted up and she had that 'boy, please, don't even try it I'm not the one' look on her face. I took heed and focused on my baby after that," he informed Tank and he could tell that put him at ease. The last thing he wanted was for Tank to second guess Von in any way because that's just not who she was.

"You reached out yet?" Tank wanted to know.

"Not yet. Ma thinks I should but I'm still on the fence about it."

"I think you should," Tank told him and from the tone of his voice, there was something behind that statement.

"She alright?" Qy asked, worried. The last thing he wanted was for something to be wrong with Chey and he wasn't there when she needed him.

"I mean yeah and no. Just reach out to her though, on the real," he heard his cousin say as he turned into his mother's driveway. He was headed to get her some more of her personal items to take them back to the hospital, but the sight of the person waiting on the porch blocked out anything else Tank was saying.

"Aye, let me hit you back," Qy said, not bothering to get a response before he hung up the phone and hopped out of his car with one of the meanest mugs he could muster up.

"Oh, big brother, you not happy to see me?" JJ taunted. His initial reason for being there was to try and make peace long enough to get what he wanted out of Qyree, but his mouth had a mind of its own.

"Nigga, you ain't no brother of mine," Qy responded. The word livid couldn't even be used to express how he was feeling at that moment.

A look of fury flashed across JJ's face and Qyree knew that he had hit a sensitive button. The day that JJ and his mother walked into that house, he could tell that they held a sense of entitlement, like they had the right to be there, but in Qyree's eyes, neither of them would be accepted and he hoped that the message was relayed loud and clear in that very moment.

Looking at Qyree was like looking into the face of Jaxon himself. Something not too many people could say about JJ. Yes, he was named after the man, but that was the only thing that he had from Jaxon besides the money that was dished out to his mother. Not only did he not look like Jaxon, as hard as he tried, he didn't act like him either. Not that too many people would think that was a good thing.

Year after year, JJ did everything he could to become the apple of his father's eye. He tried his best to emulate Jaxon, but all he heard was how he wasn't like Qyree. Qyree this and Qyree that. Qyree would have landed this artist, and Qyree earned his spot in the company. All he was reminded of was how he wasn't Qyree. This was the same thing that he had heard and felt all of his life growing up, and it would only be a matter of time before Qyree would be out of his

142

life for good. Once that happened, their father would have no choice but to praise him.

"Aye, let's be clear. You are not wanted around here, and from what I heard you never have been *wanted*. So make this the last time you in my space or it's gone be some problems," Qy warned, as he looked JJ up and down before heading in the house. He wasn't worried about anything being done to him behind his back because no matter how tough JJ may have tried to look on the outside, he could smell the scent of the punk within.

Just as he was about to close the door, the words JJ spoke next seemed to stop his world.

"I guess the way Jaxon didn't want me is the same way that you don't want Chey's baby, huh, big brother?"

-15-

"You hungry?" Von asked once Chey answered the phone. She was on her way to the doctor's office after dropping off Amir to school. Today was the day that they were going to find out what Chey was having. As excited as Chey should have been, Von knew that she couldn't enjoy it like she wanted to for two reasons. One was because she was unwed and two, because the father of her child wasn't there to share in the joy with her.

It had been so hard for both Von and Tank to keep such a big secret from Qy, but Chey begged them to keep quiet. Her mind was all over the place and the hurt she felt wouldn't allow her to call him. Fearing that he would shun her even more was something that she just couldn't face a second time. He had already done it once and she was not about to let it happen again. Her heart couldn't take it.

"You know I stay hungry, so bring me a hot cakes platter from McDonald's, a steak, egg, and cheese bagel and some orange juice. Tell them I don't want a lot of ice either," Chey

144

called out her order.

It was a good thing Von was passing by one at that moment and she was able to make the quick turn without turning her car over on two wheels. Von let her know she would be on her way in a few and they ended the call.

As Von sat in the drive thru waiting on their food, Tank crossed her mind. She thanked God every morning for sending him her way and how he just fell in synch with her and her son. Now that Chey was pregnant, it caused her to have serious baby fever, but she knew that was out of the question. If she and Tank ever got married, they wouldn't even be able to share in that process of bringing a life into the world. She was sure that he loved Amir as his own, but there was nothing like having your own child. It would be selfish of them to willingly bring a baby into their world knowing the issues it would face.

The light tapping on the window brought her out of her daydream, as she rolled it down and reached out for the bags.

"Thank you."

"You're welcome and have a great day," the cashier told her as she pulled off. It was only a short drive to the

OB/GYN office that Chey had chosen, and when she drove up she immediately spotted Chey sitting in her car.

Before she even had the chance to get out, Chey was making her way to the passenger side. Von admired Chey in her cute little emerald colored sun dress that she had dressed up with a navy blazer and accessories. Her feet were starting to swell slightly so the Toms that she wore on her feet would have to do. Her face was makeup free and her hair was curly and piled up on the top of her head.

"Morning, boo," Chey got in and hugged her quickly, before opening the bag and grabbing her food. She wasted no time digging in like she was afraid someone was going to run up on them and take it.

"You gonna stop waiting to feed my baby. Why didn't you eat something before you left home?" Von chastised.

"I ate like twenty minutes ago but I was hungry again," Chey told her, not breaking her stride. Von couldn't help but to laugh because she was definitely eating like she was pregnant.

The car was silent for a few minutes before Von spoke again.

"Tank talked to Qy yesterday," she said.

"Mm hmm."

"Mrs. Zaria is still in the hospital."

"I know, I spoke with her last night before I went to bed," Chey responded nonchalantly.

"You tell her about the baby yet?"

"Nope. And before you ask, don't. If I tell her then I know she's gonna tell Qy, and right now I need to figure things out."

"Sis, you are already six months, how much longer are you going to wait, until the child graduates?"

"Of course not. I just need a little more time." Finishing up her last bite, she took a huge gulp of her juice and opened the car door. Von understood that this conversation was not going the way that she had hoped, so she dropped it.

They grabbed their belongings, locked the car, and made their way towards the building. Taking the elevator up to the third floor, both ladies were stuck in their own thoughts but put them to the back of their minds once they got off and opened the door to the office. The excitement had resurfaced but was soon replaced by pure shock.

As soon as the door opened, everyone looked to where they were standing, Qyree and Tank included. Von could feel Chey wobble slightly, and had she not been standing there to feel the movement, she would have missed it. Qyree on the other hand didn't, and he was on his feet rushing to her right before her body went limp.

***

"I guess God is punishing me, huh?" Chey heard Qyree say the moment she opened her eyes. The faint sound of thumping filled the room as she looked around in order to remember where she was. Noticing she was in a hospital room, panic flashed across her face.

"The baby is alright. You passed out because your blood pressure was high. Your doctor rushed you over here so that you and the baby could be monitored," Qy told her.

"Where's Von?" Part of her was happy to just see him but the other part of her was still very much hurt.

"Lil' man got sick at school so Tank took her to go pick

him up. Why didn't you tell me?" he asked.

"What do you mean by God is punishing you?" Chey asked him, ignoring the question that he had just asked. She knew the reason she hid it from him would have to be discussed eventually, she just didn't want to right now.

"The baby," he started.

"You got some nerve, Qyree! Are you calling my baby punishment? Do you hear what you are saying right now?" she scoffed.

"Not like that. I mean punishing me by giving me a daughter. Lord, don't let her get treated like the women I ran through," Qy spoke. It was more to himself than her and the fact that she was having a daughter made her temporary attitude subside.

"Why didn't you tell me?" he went back to his original question.

Shrugging her shoulders, she kept her mouth closed.

"Don't you think I deserve an explanation?" he asked.

"Don't you think I deserve one too?"

His hand immediately went to his beard and he began tugging on it.

"I gave you one already."

"I know you don't mean that lie you told about me being better off without you just hours after I opened my legs to you. Do you know how that feels? Of course you don't because you're selfish, Qyree. Just like your damn no good daddy!"

"Hey! You think I wanted to leave you? You think I want to be like that man now that my eyes are finally opened to the hell he caused? I'm messed up, Cheynese! Do you know how hard it was for me once the realization hit me that I could be HIV positive? What if I had given it to you? I know it was foul to leave you right then but I wasn't thinking clearly. I felt like I didn't deserve you and before I could stand by and see you go through something like that, I walked away. Something my no good daddy didn't have the balls to man up and do. All he did was continue to drag my mother through the mud for years and not care at all about her feelings. He dragged me right along with him and made sure I kept a fresh pair of blinders on so that I couldn't see who he really was," he spoke loudly. It was loud enough to get his point across that he was mad, but not loud enough to alarm any of the staff on the other side of the door.

Chey watched as he paced the floor of her hospital room with both his hands interlocked on top of his head. The thumping noise was growing louder and faster and she didn't know why or where it was coming from. As if reading her mind, he answered the unspoken question.

"It's my baby girl's heartbeat. I need you to calm down so she will remain calm. I'm sorry for yelling and getting you upset. I had no right," he told her. He made his way back to the side of the bed where the fetal monitor was stationed and pulled his chair close and dropped his head.

"I now know that I'm negative but I'm still a wreck and until I can get myself together, Chey, I don't see how we can be together. It's not fair to you or our daughter."

"You know, the potter can't mold or reshape the clay without a wheel," she said as he looked up at her confused. "God is the potter, we are the clay, and the wheel are the ones that God uses in our lives. The wheel is in place to turn the clay in the direction that God wants it to go. It's there to keep the clay leveled and in the position that God needs it to

151

be in. The support. I don't think He brought us back together for nothing. He connected us so that we could be the support the other one needs while we continue to be reshaped by God," Chey said as she looked into his eyes.

"That's deep. Where did you hear that from?" Qy asked.

"Nobody, I just made it up sitting here and it sounded real good," she laughed. It was the first time in a long time that she was able to give a genuine laugh and it felt refreshing to her soul.

"Man, stop playing," he laughed with her. He knew that he had been missing her but it wasn't until that very moment that he knew how much. "I need my wheel back." Qyree reached up and for the first time, felt his daughter move. It felt weird but he couldn't stop the love he felt.

"You got us," Chey said touching his face. Her touch sent a wave of emotions through him as he closed his eyes and thanked God for bringing his family back together. He knew that it may not have been the way that was planned for them to be a family, but nonetheless it was a blessing and He trusted God to help him walk right for his family.

Qyree stood up and leaned over her belly and spoke,

"Qyreesha, you gotta stop kicking Mommy like that before she evicts you."

"Boy, we are not naming her no Qyreesha. I can tell all you used to mess with were ghetto girls," she said tooting up her lips.

"Word? You petty, man," he laughed.

"Yup! P-E to the T-T-Y! I'm petty all the time," Chey chanted like a cheerleader. Qy couldn't do anything but laugh before getting on the bed with her and pulling her close.

-16-

Von sat on the couch with her arms folded across her chest and her lips poked out. She couldn't believe that Tank was about to head out with Amir for the day and she wasn't allowed to go. Now that his little stomach bug was over and it was a teacher workday for the next two days, he thought his little butt was going to be spending all this free time with Tank. Shoot, she wanted some alone time with her boo, too.

"Stop throwing a fit, bae," Tank said, flopping down beside her and pulling her to him.

"Why can't we all go?" she wanted to know. She did her best to sound like a little girl hoping that would change his mind. Instead, it caused him to laugh and Amir to put in his little two cents.

"Cause it's a man thing, Ma," Amir told her, smiling. Von couldn't lie and say she wasn't happy that he had taken a liking to Tank. The way they were with one another was something that she had always wanted for her son. She knew that he had gotten the love and guidance from Terrance his whole life, and she was worried that once he was with her, he would go lacking in that area. But once again, God had a ram in the bush. *A fine ram too*, she thought.

From the confused looks on both of their faces, Von already knew that she had spoken out loud. She was really going to have to get control of her mouth and mind because they were not on one accord at all.

"Come on son, let's go," Tank said kissing Von and getting up. She couldn't help the smile that appeared hearing him call her son his son.

"Bye, Ma!" Amir yelled over his shoulder then backtracked to give his mom a hug. He was so excited about this outing that he had almost forgotten to hug and kiss her. Something he never stopped doing since she had come back into his life.

Tank made sure that Amir had his seat belt on before throwing his hand up to Von who stood in the doorway, and they pulled off. Tank had spent plenty of time with Amir but it was always with Von there. Today was the first time they would be hanging together alone and it was for a reason.

"So Mir," Tank got his attention and turned the music down.

"Yes sir?" For him to have gone through what he had at such a young age and being reunited with his mother, Amir was a well-rounded young man and Tank was proud of him. He just prayed that he could continue to be the best male figure in his life that he could be and the way God intended for him to be. That's why them being together at the moment was important. He needed to know where Amir's head was at.

"I know I haven't been in you and your mother's life for a very long period of time, but I love y'all like it's been forever," he expressed. This was out of the norm for Tank to be talking to a kid like this about their mother, but he knew it was necessary.

"You gonna marry her?" Amir wanted to know. He wasn't looking in Tank's direction. He had his eyes fixed on the passing trees and cars as he spoke.

"If that's okay with you. I mean, you been the man of the house for a minute and I can't come in just taking over without knowing how you feel about it."

"She's sick. Are you going to take care of her?" Amir turned to him with tears in his eyes. He knew they had all talked about what was going on with both Von and Tank before. Tank had even been honest and explained how he had gotten such a disease. Amir understood everything, but now that marriage was a possibility, he wanted to make sure that Tank would always be there for his mother if he married her. He didn't want her to be sick and heartbroken.

"Absolutely, son. I wouldn't dare have her be my wife and not take care of her," he told him, swiping the tear that fell from Amir's face and running his hand over his short curly hair.

Amir was silent for a few seconds and Tank could see he wanted to say something else but wasn't sure how to.

"What you thinking about lil' man?"

With hopeful eyes, Amir asked, "And me too?"

"Of course I will. That's nothing you will ever have to worry about. You are a very important part of your mom's life and now mine too. I always wanted a son and God sent me one of the best ever," Tank smiled.

"Awesome! Wait," Amir got excited and then suddenly stopped.

"How you go from Milly rockin' back to looking sad? You changed your mind about ya old man already?"

"No. Nothing like that. I was just wondering if…"

"Listen, Mir. You never have to be afraid to talk to me about anything and I will always be honest with you if you come to me, ok?"

Amir nodded his head and let out a shaky breath.

"Can I call you Dad?"

"Yo, you serious?" Tank asked. He was so happy on the inside that had he not been driving, he probably would have been hitting a quick two step. Amir once again nodded his head and waited.

"It would be an honor for you to call me dad."

"YES!" Amir yelled out and Tank laughed. Now that they had gotten that out of the way, it was time to go find his future wife her ring and get his plan moving.

***

Hours later, Von heard the front door open while she was in the kitchen, and Amir calling out to her, saying he was home. She had gotten a text from Tank letting her know to get dressed, and he would be back at eight to take them out to dinner. He was taking her back to the same restaurant that they went to on their first date, so she knew how to dress. What surprised her was that Amir was going too.

It was going on seven so she made sure to tell Amir that he needed to hurry up and get dressed. He let her know he was almost done just as the doorbell rang. She made sure that the black jumper she had on was wrinkle free and her hair was in place. Tonight she decided to wear it bone straight and swooped over to the left side of her head. On the right, close to her ear, she wore a single red rose, and her lips, along with her shoes, matched the flower perfectly.

The moment she opened the door, Tank's mouth dropped open causing her to feel a little self-conscious. Being that she was a little thicker than she had been when she was younger, there were still some days where she fought with her self-esteem. Tonight, just like on those other occasions where she second guessed herself, Tank would remind her just how beautiful she was.

"Man, baby, you look gorgeous," he smiled. The look on his face and in his eyes let her know that he meant every word.

"You don't look half bad yourself, handsome," she said, reaching out to take his hand and pull him inside. She admired the way his black suit adorned his body and fit him just right. Tank had told her to wear black and red and now she knew why. His suit was black but he wore a red shirt under his jacket that had a red handkerchief poking out of the pocket and on his feet were some red Prada loafers. God needed to distract her so that she could get her mind out of the gutter and no sooner than that thought crossed her mind, she heard steps behind her.

"I'm ready," she heard Amir saying right before she turned around to get the shock of her life. Standing there, her baby boy looked like a replica of the man that was now standing behind her. Amir was dressed just like Tank and it was the cutest thing she had ever seen.

"Dinner awaits," Tank said, reaching for her purse that was on the table beside where they stood. He knew that if he had waited any longer to leave, there was a chance that the cat would be let out of the bag, and he wanted everything to

160

be perfect.

Still in somewhat of a shock, Von got her house keys so she could lock the door and they were off. If her face hadn't been so beat, she probably would be crying one of those ugly turned up mouth cries, because the feeling of pure joy was consuming her. Instead of asking any questions, she just looked at her two men and prepared to enjoy her night.

-17-

From the looks of the restaurant parking lot, Von knew that tonight wasn't about to be as secluded as before, but she was fine with that. She felt like with them having Amir with them this time, it would be better than a normal dinner.

Once again, the valet helped her out of the car and the threesome made their way inside. Von had been waiting forever to eat so that she wouldn't ruin her appetite, so she was past ready to grub out. They followed the hostess to a table and to her surprise, not only was Qyree sitting there, but Chey was, too, looking like two love birds.

"What are y'all doing here?" Von asked as she rushed over to Chey to hug her and then to Qy.

When Chey called her the day after she had fainted and was sent to the hospital, Von shouted so hard when she told her that her and Qy were going to work things out. The happiness in her friend's voice was something that Von missed terribly and she thanked God that it was finally back.

"Well, since the two of them were acting like babies and throwing fits with one another, we never really had a chance to hang out as a group. It was either us and Qy or us and Chey. Now that they are back to acting like civilized adults, I thought it was a good time."

"I was not acting like a baby, Channing," Chey said, playfully rolling her eyes.

"Mm hmm, whatever," Tank laughed as the waiter came to take their orders. They made small talk while they waited and once the food was served, they continued to talk and laugh while Amir played on his tablet. Every once in a while, Von would catch Amir nudging Tank in the side with questionable eyes. The first few times she ignored it, but the last time she decided to tell him to stop.

"Mir, stop hitting Tank. What are you doing?"

"I'm waiting on Dad to—" he began to explain himself but was quickly cut off by his mother.

"Wait… who, Amir?" she asked in shock. The way Tank sat there smiling like a Cheshire cat instead of having the same look on his face as she did hers, threw her for a loop. When did he start calling Tank his father and how was Tank

163

alright with that?

"Before you go jumping down my lil' man's throat, it's fine. I told him he could call me that because once we say 'I do', it will be official anyway," Tank told her. Von had her eyes so focused on Amir that she hadn't noticed the ring that Tank held in his hands as he got down on one knee.

It was as if the whole restaurant had gotten quiet and was looking right in her face. She looked around the table and everyone was wearing smiles on their faces, and it was at that moment she knew that they were in on the surprise.

"Mommy, say yes!"

"Listen, baby. I know this is still new and we haven't been together that long, but I know that I love you and there is no one that I would want to spend the rest of my life with besides you. Amir already gave me his blessing."

"And I helped pick out the ring too!" Amir jumped in.

"And he picked out the ring," Tank laughed. "I'm not sure why God had us meet under these circumstances, but I know it was for a reason and I won't question His choice. I don't want you to think that me asking you this is because of our situation because it's not. If neither of us were going through this or it was just one of us, I would still feel the same way. You have already given me a son and it's only right that I have you as my wife. So Vonetta Simms, will you marry—"

"YES! OH MY GOD, YES!" Von answered before he even got the chance to finish what he was saying. The room erupted in laughs and claps as Tank slid the ring on her finger and kissed her lips. Amir jumped up and ran over to the both of them and threw his arms around them both.

Just as they were getting themselves together and the tears were being wiped from their eyes, Von heard people gasping around them. When she turned around, she understood why. Qyree was now on his knee in front of Chey.

"I don't have a speech and I don't even know how to come behind that at all," Qy started and laughed nervously. He was literally sweating bullets and his eyes looked like they were tearing up as he took Chey's hand.

"I know I messed up but it was never intentional. But once my eyes were opened I knew that I never wanted you to

165

ever hurt again, especially because of me. I'm supposed to be your protector and cover you and that's what I plan on doing. Well if you let me. Chey, baby, I love you more than I ever thought I could love a woman and I have you and God to thank for that. Will you do me the honor of being my wife so that we can bring our baby girl, Qyreesha, into this world with two of the most in love parents she could ever have?" Qy poured his heart out.

"Qyreesha? Oh God, y'all found my niece's name on a WIC voucher instead of a baby name book," Von blurted out with a straight face.

"Hush, girl!" Tank said pulling her close so that he could hide his face in her neck and laugh. His fiancée had no chill and her filter stayed broken!

"Don't hate on my baby's name," Qy said.

"That is not what we are naming our daughter, but yes, baby, I will marry you," Chey said laughing and again, the patrons celebrated with them. She didn't know how he got her ring size right, but he had done one heck of a job on picking out that joker. If she wasn't careful, she was going to need shades just to look at it.

"Looks like we have a double wedding to plan!" Von said getting hype, and high-fiving Chey.

"Well you better get to planning so we can have it before my little one gets here. I'm not bringing her into this world without her mama and daddy not being married," Qy said seriously.

"Babe, that's only three months from now. There is no way that we can do it that fast," Chey said. She didn't want to give birth out of wedlock but she had already come to terms that she would before they had gotten back together.

"I know, Chey, but I already messed up with us and I just want to make it right. You said so many times that you wanted to be married and then have babies, and although we were a little out of order, I still want to do my best to make that part come true for you."

This was why she had fallen for Qy. He may have had some difficulty knowing how to be in a relationship, but he did try when it came to her before everything happened. She looked at him and admired the growth that she saw taking place in him, and knew that he was finally walking in the purpose that he was supposed to, and she planned on being right by his side walking it with him.

As they continued their night full of laughter, love, and celebration, none of them had even noticed that they were being watched the whole time.

-18-

Qyree was headed to Chey's house for the day. He had been spending as much time with her as he could since being back together, as well as looking for a new site to start his company all over again. Initially he was going to say forget it once it burned down because the motivation was gone, but leave it up to his soon to be wife to encourage him to start again. This time he was even more excited than the last because he knew that God was in control.

Pulling in to her driveway, Qy knew that soon they would need to figure out where they were going to live full time once they got married. All of her family and friends were in Valdosta, but his mom was still in Atlanta. Thinking about Zaria and her condition made the choice a difficult one, but hopefully if everything worked out like he had planned today, then his decision would be a little easier.

Zaria and Chey had still been in contact with one another even when he and Chey weren't on speaking terms, but his mother had no idea that she was pregnant. She knew that if she had told his mother there would have been no hesitation in letting him know so that he could work things out with her. So today, once he fed both of his babies of course, they were going to go visit her together. He hoped that this visit would bring her some kind of joy and maybe even encourage her to get better. God was a healer and Qy knew that by the stripes of Jesus she was already healed. He just needed her to believe it too.

"Hey, beautiful," Qy said once he walked into Chey's house. She was dressed but was surrounded by what looked like wedding magazines and other stuff that he had no idea what it was.

"Hey, big head," he heard coming from beside her before she even had a chance to speak back.

"Bye, sis," Qy laughed.

"You so rude, Qy. Love you, sis, and I will talk to you later," Von laughed back before hanging up the phone.

"Y'all a mess. Hey, baby," Chey said, getting her things together and standing up to kiss him. As soon as his lips left her mouth, his attention was on her belly. It was like once he found out she was pregnant her stomach had grown

170

overnight.

"How's daddy's princess doing today?" he spoke to their baby like she could understand him.

"You act like she knows you already," Chey said right before their daughter began kicking like she was in a kick boxing match.

Qy looked up with a smirk on his face and said, "My baby does know her daddy! Don't get mad cause she already knows she is going to be spoiled."

Chey had no doubt about him spoiling her because it had already begun. Once they had gotten back on track, Qy went on a shopping spree and now Chey's extra room was full of baby things. He had gone out and bought her a crib, a swing, diapers, wipes, clothes, shoes, a baby tub—he saw it and he bought it.

"Let's go, I'm hungry," Chey said and pulled him towards the door and they were on their way.

IHOP was where she wanted to go and who was he to deny her what she wanted? Qy watched in awe as she enjoyed her pancakes, sirloin tips with gravy, mashed potatoes and onions, two pieces of bacon, one egg with cheese, and some strawberry French toast. There was no way that her stomach was going to be able to hold that mixture down, but so far she was enjoying it and as long as she was happy, then so was he.

They made small talk while they ate and just enjoyed one another's company. Qyree knew that this was the woman that he wanted to spend the rest of his life with, and he silently thanked God for bringing her back to him. Once they were in the car and on the road headed to see his mother, Chey's phone rang. It was a number that had looked familiar but she couldn't put her finger on it, so she declined it only for it to call right back.

"Gone and answer your boyfriend Grady, you know that's him calling you and tell him we gone need that social security check on the third. These pampers ain't cheap," Qyree joked.

"You so crazy. Hello?" she answered.

"Chey?" said the familiar voice.

"Yes, this is Chey. Mama Gladys?"

"It's been so long you don't know my voice anymore?" Gladys laughed.

"I'm sorry it has been a long time, but that's my fault. How are you and Papa Cecil doing?"

"Oh baby, that's ok. I know you have been a busy woman but Francine keeps me updated on how well you are doing. And that old coon is fine. Still thinking he the best thing smokin' since sliced bread ya' kno'," she laughed.

"That's 'cause I am!" Chey heard him in the background and fell out laughing right before she heard the sounds of a baby crying.

"See what you did with that big mouth, done woke this here child up and I just got him to go back to sleep." It took a few minutes to get the baby calm before Chey heard Gladys speak again.

"Lord have mercy, give me strength 'cause I'm too old for this. Chey, baby, I was calling to see if by any chance you have spoken to or seen that granddaughter of mine."

It was at that moment that Chey knew who the crying baby belonged to.

173

"Not since she popped up at church about a month ago," Chey told her as she looked over at Qy who was visibly upset. As soon as he had found out about Natalia confronting her, he wanted to go by and let her have it but she wouldn't let him. So he called Von instead. That fool had come to her house in some sweats, tennis shoes, and a face full of Vaseline. The scene wasn't funny then because she was trying to calm everyone down, but as soon as everything blew over, she laughed so hard she peed in her pants.

"She did what?" Gladys yelled bringing her back to the conversation at hand.

"Yeah, she came in talking about I owed her an apology for stealing her man or whatever because I'm with Qy. Mama was about to let her have it but she left," Chey explained.

"And she should have beat the brakes off of her for all of this foolishness she's causing. Coming by here out of the blue with a baby and ain't been back to get him since. I'm too old for this and she acting just like her mama did."

Chey couldn't believe what she was hearing but it didn't really surprise her. That was Natalia for you. She just hated that now she had a baby in this world who was probably sick, too, and needed the proper care, but his mother was out running behind men that didn't want her. It was sad. Even though she was upset with Natalia, she still prayed for her nightly that God would cover her and help her. The word says to bless those who curse you and pray for those who mistreat you, and that was what Chey did. No matter how much her flesh wanted to get back at Natalia, she just couldn't fight evil with evil.

"I'm sorry you're going through this, Mama Gladys, and if I come across where she may be, I will definitely let you know."

"Well thank you, baby. If I don't hear something from her soon, then I'm gonna have to get child welfare involved. This baby needs special care and you know that if Cecil and I were a little younger, then we would keep him with no problem. It's just hard with all of the challenges he's gonna face with his little cute self," Gladys said as she wiped a tear from her eye. It hurt her to her heart to know this baby was going to struggle in life because his mama was selfish. Not only was he born with a deadly disease and needed medicines, he had a few birth defects that would hinder him some as well when it came to learning.

Gladys figured that instead of Natalia getting the proper care for both herself and her child, she was out running behind a man, or men for that matter. Now she had brought this baby in to the world for him to struggle. She knew it was possible that he could have been born just fine with nothing at all wrong, if she had done what a mother should but she didn't. It was mothers like her that made Gladys feel like not all women should have children. There were women every day praying for a baby while others get pregnant and treated the child any kind of way. It just didn't make sense to her.

After saying their goodbyes and hanging up, Chey filled Qy in with everything that was said. He knew Natalia wasn't wrapped too tight before, but he really knew she was crazy then and was glad that he had dodged that ball. But just as he pulled up to the hospital and parked, he didn't know if he would be as lucky to dodge the one that was headed in his direction.

Qyree groaned inwardly as he made his way around the car to help Chey out but right before he could get her door open, the ball dropped.

"REE!" Trinity called out. He was praying that she didn't spot him because if she did, he knew she was going to show out. That's just what she did.

Letting the handle go, he quickly turned around and hoped he could get rid of her before Chey got upset or Trinity showed her butt once again in public. He had no idea how Chey would react and for the first time, he was slightly nervous.

"What Trinity?" he asked as he brought his hand across his face.

"*What Trinity?*" she mocked. "You just leave me almost a year ago and all you got to say is what Trinity?"

Instead of responding, he just looked at her until a car door shutting caught both of their attention. It didn't dawn on him that it was his car door until he heard Chey speak.

"Baby, we have got to get that door fixed or either just a new car altogether before the baby comes," Chey said walking up to him with a smile on her face. He looked down and realized that he had his body pressed up against the passenger door, preventing Chey from getting out because he wanted her to stay put, but this woman had carried her and

177

her seven-month pregnant self, clean over to the driver's side and got out.

"Yea, ahem, yeah, how about we just get a new one instead. New baby, new beginnings, so why not a new car?" he smiled. Qy was about three and a half seconds away from having an accident in his pants because he was nervous. It may have been funny any other time knowing that the one and only Qyree Reeves had the bubble guts because he was being confronted by a woman, but it just wasn't funny right then.

"Oh hi, I'm Chey, and you are?" Chey said calmly. She had peeped game as soon as Qy suddenly stopped shy of opening her door. She then leaned her seat back just a little so she could see out of the back window and view what he was looking at.

The moment she saw the woman she knew it had to be one of his old flings. She couldn't lie, the girl was beautiful, but that didn't move or intimidate her one bit. The outfit she had on was cute and her hair was styled to perfection, but the attitude she had made her so unattractive. Call it conceit, arrogance, or confident, whatever you like, but Chey knew that she was a definite upgrade from the woman who was

178

rolling her neck and poppin' her gum in her man's face. That's why she smoothly eased over the console and exited the other side. Who was she kidding? She had struggled to make sure she didn't hit her stomach or cause the car to shake too much because that would draw attention; before she had the chance to get out. Once she made it over, she had to take a few seconds to breathe because that task had her winded.

Not bothering to respond, Trinity looked Chey up and down and turned up her nose. Not because Chey was ugly or anything, as a matter of fact, Trinity thought she was gorgeous. But, she turned her nose up because of the way that Qyree was protecting her and seeing the love that was clearly evident in his eyes when he looked at her. It wasn't until Chey brought her hand to her very noticeable baby bump with her engagement ring shining brightly that Trinity got mad.

She had been messing around with Qy off and on for three years up until the night he left her while she was running behind his car after fighting that Dominican chick. From that day on, she had been trying to get in touch with him, but obviously he had her number blocked. He wanted to play her so she would play him right back, or so she thought.

"I'm Trinity. Qyree's girlfriend," she said crossing her arms over her chest like she had just done something. She was in the right place for medical attention because the daggers that Qyree was throwing from his eyes in her direction were sure to kill her.

"Ohhhhh, this is the one that you beeeen blocked, bae? The one that was always running behind your car when you would leave her," Chey laughed. Qy looked at his woman in shock because he had never told her about Trinity and Trinity looked like she wished she had a rock to go hide under.

"Trinity, hun, you're not his girlfriend, and any little shot you take at me will not affect me. I know who I have in Qyree and I know all about the boy he used to be when he was messing with you. He's a full grown man now and about to be a husband as well as a father, and he doesn't have time to play games. You are a beautiful girl and you deserve someone that will treat you like the queen that you are. It just won't be this one," she said pointing at Qy. "You have a blessed day now, alright?"

The look on Qyree's face said it all as he grabbed Chey's hand and moved around Trinity and they began to walk towards the entrance. Not one time did Chey raise her voice or act out of character, and that was so attractive to him. He just knew that once he heard that car door close and then heard her voice, that it was about to be a situation. But, she carried herself with so much class he was speechless. It was definitely something he wasn't use to. Normally, the women he had been with in the past would be in the middle of a screaming match or fighting by now, and he would have been in his car pulling off, but not this time.

"What?" Chey asked as she pressed the button for the elevator doors to close. Qy was looking at her like she was a rare breed or something.

"Man, Chey, when I heard you get out that car on the other side I swear I almost messed up my drawers," he told her and she laughed.

"Why?"

"I don't know. It was different this time being confronted by one woman while I was with another one. Usually I don't even care about a confrontation, but the last thing I want now is for my past to come back and mess up what we have," he told her honestly, pulling her close to him. "I respect you too much to embarrass you out here like that."

"I know, Qy, that's why I didn't go off on her. For one, Tank already told me you cut off everybody. Even while we were apart, you didn't mess with anyone and that had a lot to do with me being able to take you back. To know that you still respect, not just me but yourself while we weren't together, really showed me your growth. And two, I could look at her and tell that she was lost. Until she finds out her true worth, she will just move on to the next man to try and find fulfillment. If I had gone off on her like she wanted and expected me to, then she would have known that she could keep trying me about mine. She would go out of her way to try and tear us apart because that would have said to her that I was intimidated. Ain't no weak link this way boo 'cause I'm secure about mine. Besides, a queen never gets off of her throne to address a peasant."

"My Queen you definitely are," Qy said as he admired her. *God broke the mold with this one*, he thought as they headed to their destination hand in hand.

There was so much noise coming from one side of the hospital floor that Qyree and Chey had just stepped off on. They couldn't tell where exactly it was, but the closer they moved in the direction of Zaria's room, the louder it got.

Letting go of Chey's hand, he told her to stay where she was. If anything was going down, the last thing he wanted was for her to get pulled with him and get hurt. As soon as he bent the corner, he saw about three security officers surrounding a figure across from Zaria's room that he couldn't make out too well, because they were blocking him and he heard his mother having one of her coughing spells. Instead of worrying about who they had detained right then, his main concern was checking to make sure she was okay.

"Ma, you alright?" he asked, running up to her bedside. That same nurse Brittanie that seemed to always be there when he came, was by her side, and as soon as she saw him, she couldn't help but to smile. Even if he had been interested in her, which he wasn't, that would have definitely turned him off. She was too busy skinning and grinning in his face instead of doing her job and helping his mother.

Zaria coughed a few more times and was finally able to take a breath and calm herself down as she held on to his forearm. He looked at her and could feel his heart breaking as he took in her appearance. Her skin was ashy and lackluster, she was slowly losing weight, and her eyes showed so much pain in them when she looked at him.

Before either of them could speak, they heard a gasp behind them and he turned to see Chey standing by the door. Tears were already forming in her eyes and Qy began to second guess if it was a good idea bringing her here. He had hoped her showing up and letting Zaria know she was about to be a grandmother would give her some type of fight, but the last thing he wanted was for Chey to get upset and upset the baby.

"I'll go get you some more water, Mrs. Reeves, along with your medicine," Brittanie said. That smile she had flashed at Qy was no longer there once Chey came in the room, but Chey was too focused on his mother to pay any attention to the nurse.

"Oh my God, Ma," Chey said rushing over to be beside

184

Zaria. From the beginning, Zaria had taken a genuine liking to Chey and had started looking at her as her daughter. That's why she fought so hard to try and get them back together and kept communication open with her. Looking down, she reached out and touched Chey's stomach at the very moment the baby kicked, causing Zaria to cover her mouth as the tears flowed down her face.

"I'm so sorry I didn't tell you before now, Ma. I was so caught up in my own feelings that I didn't want you to tell Qy because I knew you wouldn't keep it a secret. Now I wished I had. Maybe you would still fight to be here with us. Please don't give up just yet. You have to meet your granddaughter," Chey cried as she laid her head gently on Zaria's shoulder.

Qyree stood there not knowing what to do besides pray, so that's what he did until Brittanie came back in with the water and medicine. It had been months since she had taken anything that could possibly help her to get better. There had been many days that he had begged her to take it but she had refused. Turning to leave back out, the nurse rolled her eyes at Qy and shut the door.

Another one bites the dust.

"It's not too late. We know you are a miracle worker, God. All things are possible with you and you can't fail nor are you like man that you shall lie. It says in your word that by the stripes of Jesus we are healed and I believe that with my whole heart as I stand in the gap for your servant and daughter right now. Give Zaria a fresh wind and a new mind to know that she can prosper and live a long happy life. So many years she has had to fight but has been so distracted and didn't remember that we don't fight against flesh and blood. We fight against principalities, powers, and rulers of an unseen world. But you see all, God. Fight this battle for her from the top of her head to the soles of her feet. We decree that it is so in the mighty and matchless name of Jesus, Amen."

"Amen," everyone said including the nurse who had returned and two of the security officers no one knew was there.

As soon as Chey had finished her prayer and sat up, Zaria reached over and began taking everything she needed to help her to get better. There may not have been a cure for what she had, but she wasn't about to just lay there and wait for her life to end any longer. She had a son, a daughter-in-law, and a grandbaby that needed her and she was going to do everything she could to get back to where she needed to be.

-20-

Jaxon couldn't believe his eyes when he walked into the hospital room and saw Zaria lying there looking the way that she was. The once vibrant vixen he had known for all of those years had vanished and for what? Because she just wouldn't let him do him.

When he had first met Zaria back in the 10th grade, every boy in school wanted her but they only wanted one thing and she wasn't having it. At that time, that was all he wanted too, but once she showed interest in him as well, she still made him work for it. After a while of them dating steady, she was finally his and that included her body too.

Jaxon's mother had died when he was younger so he didn't have that female there to tell him how to treat a woman, so he was just winging it. He knew the type of man that his father was, but Zaria made him want to be different. She was much like what Chey was to his son when he thought about it.

Zaria was good for him and she pushed him to be a better young man. All of the dreams and aspirations that he had about becoming this big time music exec and having his own company sounded crazy to everyone else, but not to Zaria. She encouraged him and made sure to stand by him every step of the way. That was until the fast life blinded him.

By then, they had already had Qyree and Zaria was adamant about not having a nanny raising their son in his early years. She wanted to be a hands on mother and wanted him to be that hands on father, but that would only cramp his style. The more that Zaria was away, his father was able to get in his ear, telling him how he could have him a good wife at home and his little play things outside that she didn't have to know about. Only Jaxon was a flashy man and loved to show off what he had. The money had changed him.

Jaxon no longer cared about anyone but himself and although he did love his wife and son, he loved his money and status more. The higher he climbed in his career meant that more women were coming his way, and he welcomed them with opened arms. At first, he tried to hide them but after about the fourth one came ringing his bell and Zaria had to deal with yet another one but she still didn't bother to leave, he felt like…why stop? If she wasn't going to respect herself anymore, then why should he? Zaria had let her self-respect go when that was the very thing that had drawn him to her in the first place.

"Excuse me, sir, can I help you?" he heard from behind him. He was so caught up in his thoughts that he had forgotten he was still standing in front of his wife's door but had yet to go in.

He looked the young nurse up and down and licked his lips seductively. The way that he imagined her body looked under the scrubs she was wearing had him ready to get her number and take her out later. Yeah she looked to be around his son's age but he liked them young. The younger the better.

"Go on, Brittanie, you don't want my husband. If he doesn't get some medicines in him soon he's going to be lying right next to me, right honey?" she said sarcastically. That caused the nurse to turn fast on her heels in the other direction. She had figured that if she couldn't have the son, she could definitely bag his father, but after that little revelation she would gladly pass. Brittanie had her fair share of men and normally she could look at someone and tell if

190

they were sick or not, but she had missed it with that one. He was so fine and built that she thought there was no way that he was walking around with anything, but let his wife tell it he was, and she believed her.

Jaxon's eyes had turned red and he was as hot as fire at the sound of her once again saying that he had AIDS. No, he hadn't gone to the doctor yet, but he had never felt better. That was the only reason why that he was making this visit was to show Zaria how good he looked. She could fool everyone else into thinking she had gotten sick because of him, but he knew better. He would bet any amount of money that she had called herself trying to get back at him by sleeping with someone else and that one slipup had cost the woman her life.

"Why are you here?" Zaria asked with her voice cracking. Just looking at her husband made her want to cry as all of the good memories played in her mind but they were instantly followed by all of the memories of the hell he had caused everyone around him.

"I'm just here so you can see how good I look. Do I look like a dying man to you?" he asked, straightening his tie with a sly smirk on his face. She thought she was hurting him but

191

he was showing her that he would always remain on top.

"Baby, even the devil used to be an angel of light. How you think he goes around deceiving people? You better believe he makes himself or the temptation look and smell real good. I'm sure you know all about that. The holes you dip in smelled real good but one of them jokers was just as rotten. Don't worry though, you've always been in pretty good health so it might just be taking its time to tear up that immune system. Or God is just going to make you suffer later," she shrugged. That one motion paired with everything she had just said to him, sent him over the edge and before he knew it, his hands were around her throat.

Zaria didn't even have any fight left in her and Jaxon would put her right on out of her misery. He had killed her spirit long ago, so she might as well let him take the rest of her, so she didn't even fight back. Before she knew it, Jaxon was being pulled away from her by three security guards. Once his hands were removed from her throat, she couldn't get the coughing to stop when her nurse rushed to her side and before long Qyree was making his way to her.

It was then that Jaxon knew he needed to get out of there because if Qyree had found him there, he may very well be lying on a stretcher, but it wouldn't be beside Zaria but down in the morgue. He apologized quickly and was able to leave. They let him know that if he returned they would make sure to get the police involved the next time. One of the guards recognized who he was and that was the only reason he had gotten that pass. Now here he was pulling up to one of his many houses that no one knew about, or so he thought.

-21-

Toni was breaking all kinds of laws as she flew down the streets of Atlanta. She was surprised she hadn't been pulled over yet, but she had to get to her son. JJ wasn't stable and she knew that if she didn't find him, it could be a bad ending for someone. She had been keeping up with him by the tracker that she had on his car, but it was now stopped at an address that she was unfamiliar with. It was about forty-five minutes outside of the city and she had just gotten in her car.

"Hello? JJ, baby, where are you?" she asked once he picked up his phone. She did her best to sound calm as she whizzed past cars with their horns blaring.

"I'm good, Ma. Don't worry, it will all be over soon," he responded but he didn't sound right. Something in his voice told Toni that something was terribly wrong.

"What will all be over soon?"

"You were right, Ma, about the baby. He wasn't mine," JJ said right before he burst out crying.

Toni listened to her only son sobbing and it scared her so bad that her eyes had begun to water causing her to almost sideswipe a parked car.

"Oh shoot!" she yelled out.

"I already did."

"Wait, what? JJ, what are you talking about?" she panicked.

"I already shot her," he said calmly. Way too calmly for her.

"JJ, who did you shoot, baby? Tell Mommy so I can come and help you."

"NO! I don't want you to see her like this. You have to wait to see her after they reconstruct her face. Not like this. Not like this. Not like this," he repeated over and over again.

"OH GOD, JJ WHAT DID YOU DO?! WHO DID YOU SHOOT? TELL ME RIGHT NOW!"

"I'm sorry, Mommy," he said sounding like he was a little boy. It was something he would always do when she would yell or fuss at him for misbehaving.

That was why she needed Jaxon to be in his life because she knew he had mental problems and she had always thought that Jaxon would be able to help him. The times that Jaxon would spend the night or be around JJ for days at a time, she never had to worry about JJ showing out. Just as soon as Jaxon would leave though, she had a time getting JJ back under control. This was the reason she fought so hard for him to have a position at the company.

It all worked out when Toni went to Jaxon on behalf of her son and put all kinds of things in his head that wasn't true. Things like how she had heard that Qy was going to leave the company and that he was going to blackball Jaxon in the industry. Just a whole bunch of negative things that weren't true about Qy. For a while, she was worried that her trick hadn't worked until JJ called her one day screaming about how he was going to be able to work with his dad, but it would take a little while. Jaxon had to make sure that all of the artists Qyree was working to get would sign before he filled the position. Just the fact that he was going to be with his father on the regular, caused JJ to make a significant change mentally as he waited for the day he could fill Qyree's position.

The day Toni and JJ had been waiting for had finally come the night everyone was at Jaxon's house. She was a little worried about showing up at first because it wasn't Jaxon who had called her and invited her over, but it was Zaria who made the call. Once they had gotten there, confusion and shock was evident on Qyree's face, but not Zaria's or Jaxon's. The only one in that house that was in the dark about JJ was Qy, and it made the announcement of JJ taking the position Qy should rightly have that much sweeter. Toni couldn't enjoy the moment for very long however. After the announcement, Zaria revealed what she had to say. It felt like no matter what, that woman would always have one up on her but she had no one to blame but herself.

It wasn't until Qyree was gone from Hype Lyfe and was actually planning to start his own business is when things with JJ really hit the fan. JJ couldn't perform like he was supposed to and it didn't take long for artists to back out of working with Hype Life as a company, and JJ had no idea how to make them stay. Jaxon may have gotten the company off the ground, but it was because of his son, Qyree, that the company was thriving the way it was. It was just something about Qy that made him a good fit for that industry.

When Jaxon came to JJ about all the mistakes he had made dealing with the artists, he almost went over the deep end again. It wasn't until JJ brought back evidence of burning down Qyree's new studio that Jaxon became happy with him again. Jaxon was happier than a fat baby in a bakery but just like before, that happiness didn't last long until finally JJ was fired. Ever since then, Toni had to stay on top of him at every turn because she knew that something like this was bound to happen.

"I gotta go, he's here!" was all Toni heard before the call ended. She tried calling back to back but kept getting his voicemail.

Looking on the tablet beside her on the seat, she saw that his car still hadn't moved so she did the only thing that she could.

"Hello, 9-1-1, what is your emergency?"

"Yes, I think my son has killed someone and is about to shoot someone else," she told the operator before rattling off the address she had. She knew that God may not be on the main line right then for her, but she prayed that either she or

198

the police got to where JJ was before it was too late.

-22-

Hearing the T-Mobile generic ringtone caused Jaxon to stop in his tracks the moment he walked in his house. He was so tired mentally that he didn't even bother to lock the door behind him. No one was supposed to be there because not a soul knew about this place. He had been so into his thoughts that he wasn't even paying attention to the outside of the house to see if anything was out of place. Now he wished that he had.

"Come on in, *Dad*," he heard coming from around the corner. He knew good and well that JJ wasn't in his house, but more importantly how did he find it?

"How did you…" Jaxon began and trailed off once he entered his living room. The sight before him made his stomach churn instantly and it took all of the strength that he had to keep his stomach contents down.

Before him was Natalia in a pool of her own blood, with her long hair covering her face. Just like JJ had been

200

following Jaxon he was on the lookout for Natalia as well. It just so happened to be his lucky day when he saw her coming out of a nearby corner store. Before she had a chance to react he had already knocked her out cold and placed her in the back of his car. It was dark out so he knew that no one saw him before he took off to Jaxon's house. He had wanted to wait and kill them both but she had woken up and tried to get away so he shot her and waited for his next victim.

"Oh my God!" Jaxon said.

"Hmm, God? You know Him? I wonder if He knows you," JJ said as he tapped the barrel of the gun against his own temple as if he was thinking long and hard.

"Come on, son, don't do this," Jaxon pleaded, causing him to spin around with his face contorted.

"So nowwwwww I'm your son, huh? Was I your son when you fired me? Or better yet, was I your son on the nights that you didn't come home to me and mommy? Was I your son when you were with Qyree and teaching him how to be a man? WAS I YOUR SON THEN?!" JJ shouted.

Jaxon had no idea what to do because clearly JJ was not stable. Maybe if he had spent more time around him he

201

would have known how to handle the situation in front of him. Before he could open his mouth, the front door burst open and he heard footsteps running towards him. He hoped it was the police coming to help him, but that notion flew out the window the moment Toni's face appeared.

"Mommy?"

"Yes, baby, it's me," Toni said as she tried to inch her way towards her son. She was so focused on him she didn't even realize that she was about to step on Natalia until JJ yelled.

"DON'T YOU DARE STEP ON HER!"

"JESUS!" she shouted right before she broke down crying.

"It's the sweetest name I know," JJ sang out as if he was in church. "Yeah heee. Something about the name Jesus. It is the sweetest name I know. Some people say I'm crazy but…"

"JJ, stop it baby," Toni tried her best to bring him back. He was about to go into the whole rendition of Kirk Franklin's song "Something About The Name Jesus" featuring The Rance Allen Group.

"Stop what, mother? Maybe if you had stopped playing with people years ago then you would have told Jaxon that I'm not really his son!" JJ blurted out.

"What?" Jaxon said looking over at Toni who was now nothing but tears. Everyone knew that JJ didn't look like Jaxon or Qyree, but was the spitting image of his mother. Jaxon thought that he had Toni's nose so wide open back then that he never thought she would ever step out on him. For the life of Toni, she had no idea how JJ knew about this secret and unfortunately she never would.

POW!

Jaxon watched as Toni's body hit the floor and this time he couldn't hold his stomach together. It took him a few minutes to be able to get himself together but he made sure to keep his eyes on JJ.

"She lied to me! She lied to me just like Natalia," JJ said barely above a whisper. JJ didn't even remember what he was doing when he stumbled across paperwork that looked like DNA documents. Taking the time to study them he saw that those results revealed that Jaxon was excluded from

203

being his father. It was then that he knew eventually his mother would have to be eliminated too.

"I'm sorry," was the only thing that Jaxon could think to say at that moment.

"You could have saved me, Daddy," JJ said. Now Jaxon knew good and well that this boy admitted that he knew he was not his father, and here he was back to calling him daddy again.

"You know you lied too. See what happens to people that lie?" JJ said as he raised his gun and pointed it at Jaxon.

"No...no...no... I never lied to you. I thought you were my son all this time."

"You did lie to me! Every time I asked you would you come back what did you say?!" JJ asked with tears falling from his eyes.

"I said I would be back."

"Did you come back?"

"No."

"What did you tell me when I asked why you loved

Qyree more?"

"I-I-I-I said, um, that, that I didn't love him more and I loved you both the same," Jaxon stuttered.

"Lie, lie, lie! If you loved us the same, you would have treated us the same but you didn't. Because of you, everybody you ever claimed to love will die. If not from that disease you been passing around then by my hands," JJ said right before two shots rang out and a swarm of police rushed in. They may have shot him with bean bag rounds, but Jaxon wasn't so lucky.

JJ didn't feel one thing for anyone that he had just hurt as he was handcuffed. They had all hurt him in one way or another. The only person he was mad that he didn't get was Qyree, but he could live with that. He was probably lied to just like him. He wasn't even paying attention as the officer read him his rights and placed him in the back of the police car. And to think that all of this hell started because of the so called heaven between a woman's thighs.

-23-

To say that Qyree was mad once his mother and the security guards told him what had happened between his father and mother was an understatement. He was so focused on his mother doing all of that coughing when they had arrived earlier that he hadn't had a second thought about the man who was being held by the security guards. It had taken them all quite a while to get him calm enough to where he would stop threatening to leave the hospital. There was no telling what could have happened to him if he had gone to find that man.

Once he was finally calm and in a better head space, they talked about everything under the sun and even baby names with his mother. To see the light that was once in her eyes return gave Qyree hope that everything would work out just fine for her. His mother's doctor told them that usually cases like hers didn't end well, but he was optimistic and he was saved. He had all the faith in not only natural medicine, but that heavenly healing that he knew could take place.

"We are not naming this baby no Qyreesha," Chey said, rolling her eyes.

"Lord, don't tell me that's what you really want to name my grandbaby, Qy," Zaria said laughing.

"What's wrong with that name?"

"It's ratchet!" Chey and Zaria said at the same time.

"Whatever," he said with a fake attitude.

"What about Harmony? That's exactly what she will be bringing into our lives. I'm sure there are more trials coming our way but this little princess will definitely bring us together in peace," Zaria suggested.

"That's beautiful," Chey said smiling.

"I can dig that," Qy agreed.

Just as they were about to get ready to go because both Zaria and Chey were getting tired, Chey felt a sharp pain in the lower part of her abdomen.

"Oomph!" she winched in pain and held her stomach.

"Baby, you alright?" Qyree ran over to her in a panic but

Zaria was already pressing the button for the nurse.

"I just stood up too fast that's all," she said before taking a step and experiencing one of the biggest pains in her life; and at the same time, a big gush of water came from between her legs. It was as if time stood still and sped up all at the same time.

There were doctors and nurses moving in every direction while Qyree tried to make sure he called her parents along with Von and Tank. He prayed that they all would get there before his daughter was born because there was no way to stop her since Chey's water had broken. Qy was a wreck because he had just found out a little over a month ago that he was going to be a father, and here she was making her grand entrance way too early. Just as he was about to walk out of his mother's room, the breaking news that was being broadcast from the local news station made his world stop.

"We are live at the scene of what looks to be an apparent triple homicide. Police have confirmed that two women were dead on arrival along with a male victim," the news anchor stated then paused as if she was receiving new information into her headset before speaking again.

"It was just confirmed that the third victim is still alive but is in critical condition and is none other than Hype Lyfe Records CEO Jaxon Reeves. The suspect that is still here on the scene is known as his son, a Mr. Jaxon Reeves, Jr. That is all of the information that we have at this time, but once we have more we will be back with a live update. Back to you guys in the studio."

"Go be with Chey and my grandbaby. I will be praying. For everyone," Zaria said. Qy stood there a few seconds longer to make sure that she was going to be okay and when he saw her square her shoulders back and hold her head high, he knew she was going to be okay until he got back. That was the strength that he had always prayed that he would see in his mother again since she had been in the hospital, and God had just answered his prayer in that instant.

-24-

"Qyree Jayceon Reeves, I swear to God you better not come near me right now! You did this to me with your ugly self and pretty eyes. I knew I should have given you all the wrong answers back in college when I was tutoring so you couldn't graduate!" Chey ranted as everyone around her laughed.

"Don't worry, son, this isn't the worst that I've heard before," the doctor said to him and he nervously moved around to the other side of the bed.

"I'm sorry, Qy," Chey pouted as she grabbed his hand and pulled him near. He was a little hesitant because he felt like she was going to hit him once he got close to her. Then the tears started falling from her eyes and that let him know that no amount of pain she could deliver to him could possibly be worse than what she was feeling. So if she needed to punch, pinch, or grab him, he would let her, but only for the time she was in labor. She better not even think about it once this was all over.

"Well you are going to be here a little while. Even though your water has broken you are still only at four centimeters. I'll get you something for the pain if you'd like and come back and check on you in about an hour," Dr. Montgomery said before he threw his gloves in the trash, signed off on something the nurse was holding, and walked out of the room.

"I'll be right back with your pain meds," her nurse told her.

"It won't hurt her will it? I mean, especially with her being early and all?" Qy wanted to know. The last thing he wanted was for his little princess to be born with any problems.

"Oh no, it won't. This is safe and she's not getting too much. We are definitely going to keep a close eye on her but as of right now, baby's heart rate is very good to be so early. I'll be right back," she explained before she walked out.

"I like her better than your mother's nurse. At least she wasn't trying to be all in your face and could do her job," Chey said rolling her eyes hard at him. He couldn't help but laugh because he didn't even realize she had peeped ol' girl earlier. Chey didn't miss nothing.

"Aww, my boo-boo jealous?" he teased before another contraction hit.

"Get away from me with your ugly self, Qy! Ohhh, I can't stand you."

"Hold on, she will be your best friend again in just a few seconds," Ms. Kathy told him. He wished whatever she was giving Chey would hurry up and kick in because right then, she was giving him a serious side eye. She opened her mouth to say something then closed it back quickly before finally speaking.

"I love you so much, Qy," she said as her eyes slowly closed.

"See, I told you."

"Can I get some of that to take home with us just in case she gets mad again?" he asked seriously.

"I hear you, Qy," Chey said but with a smile on her face.

"Y'all are too cute. How long have you two been married?" Ms. Kathy asked. It was as if the realization had hit them at the same time that she would be having the baby and they weren't married yet.

"We are still engaged," Qy said sadly as he wiped the tear from Chey's face. He knew how much she wanted to be married before the baby, but there was no way that they would be able to do it now.

"Have you already filled out the application for marriage?" she asked them.

"Yeah. We did that the other day and got our license, but it's not valid until we have the wedding."

"Well, all you need is someone ordained to marry you then, don't you?" she said as if she had solved the world's hardest mystery.

At that very moment, the door to the room they were in flew open and in ran Francine and Davis.

"My baby is about to have a baby!" Francine cried causing Chey to look at her strange.

"What's wrong, punkin? Why you looking like that?" her grandfather Davis asked looking worried.

"Mebout tohaveababy and, and, and, I'm not married to Qyree ugly self," she cried with her words running together.

"It's the medicine I just gave her so she's a little woozy," Ms. Kathy told them and they relaxed.

Before they knew it, Chey was snoring loudly, and finally comfortable. Ms. Kathy monitored the baby for a little while longer before leaving the family to themselves for a while.

"What's on your mind young man?" Davis asked Qy as Francine called all of the church members she could to let them to know to pray for a healthy and safe delivery.

"I messed up. I went and got her pregnant and now I don't even have time to marry her and make it right," he said with his head down.

"You know, son, at first I wanted to find you and give you a piece of my mind but then that old fine thing over there had to sit me down and get me together. I ain't been saved all my life either. I was wild back in my day. Tried to sow as many oats as I could," Davis told Qy.

"And I chopped them weeds ret on down too!" Francine

jumped in causing Qy to laugh. Those two were a trip.

"Hush up, woman. Anyway, let me make this quick before she gets mad. Have you repented?"

"Yes, sir."

"Well if you asked for God's forgiveness from the heart, then His grace is sufficient enough. We all have been guilty of condemning ourselves long after God has forgiven us instead of resting in that forgiveness. The spirit is willing but the flesh is weak, son, so you had a moment of weakness that resulted in this baby about to be born but she is a blessing. And you are a blessing to us as well. I know how happy you make my baby over there and as long as you treat her right, I will be right there to have your back," Davis told him with a strong pat on the back.

That one gesture broke down walls that Qyree didn't even know he had up as the water began to flow from his eyes. Davis understood what he needed and it was just that fatherly touch, so he held him and let him cry. Men always tried to hold things inside instead of getting their release. It didn't mean that they were less than just because they showed emotions, but they are human. Once they get it out, they are stronger to fight another day.

"I'm proud of you, son, I really am."

"Thank you for that," Qy said as the women watched them with tears in their eyes as another pain hit Chey.

"Mama, he's so ugly!" she cried as the nurse came back in to check her. Before the door could close all the way, Von and Amir came through, followed by Tank pushing Zaria in a wheelchair.

"Oh good, we got here right in time! Here is the marriage license and Pop, here is your stuff that you told me to get," Von said handing Davis everything he had asked for. He was glad that he had advised them to go ahead and get everything done just in case something like this happened.

"It's always better to be prepared just in case. So do we have the rings?"

"Yep, right here," Tank said as he moved beside Qy and dapped him up.

"Thanks, bruh."

"You already know I got you."

"I hate to rush you guys but this little one is ready to come out so we may want to get on with this real fast because I can see her beginning to crown," Dr. Montgomery said, sitting right in front of where Chey was propped up.

Davis said a quick prayer of blessing over their marriage before he started and broke a record for the fastest wedding ever. There were a few times that he had to pause in order for Chey to push through the contractions but they were quickly pronounced husband and wife. Just as Qy leaned down to kiss Chey, she pushed one last time before hearing one of the most precious sounds ever.

"Well look what we have here. Happy birthday, beautiful girl. Would you like to cut the cord, Dad?" the doctor asked.

Qy had to wipe his eyes a few times before he took the surgical scissors and clamped down where he was instructed to do so. He was so overwhelmed with emotions because he had become a dad and a husband literally at the same time. Looking down into Harmony's face as she lay quietly on Chey's chest like she was trying to figure everyone out, he felt his heart swell with pride as he made a promise that he knew he would have no trouble keeping.

"I'm gonna be the best daddy ever to you princess. I promise," he told her before kissing her chubby cheek and then turning to Chey. "And I'm gonna be the best husband ever to you my queen, I promise."

"I already know you are. I love you, Qy," she said before kissing his lips.

"Y'all are sooo cute!" Von said all loud and ghetto, causing everyone to laugh. In that room, Qy had everyone that he needed in his life and everything felt right. Regardless of the broadcast that he had heard a few hours before, he was happy, and no matter if Jaxon survived his ordeal or not, Qy still loved him and was at peace. His only prayer was that Jaxon had been able to find that peace as well.

-Epilogue-

Two years later...

Chey used the tissue in her hand to pat at her eyes so that she wouldn't ruin her makeup. The last thing she wanted to do was to show up at her husband's event looking like a drunk raccoon, but she needed to do this before they headed to their destination.

"You alright, baby?" Qy asked as he reached over to take her hand in his as he pulled away from the marker and headed towards the front of the cemetery.

All she could do was shake her head because if she had spoken right then, she would be sure that her makeup would be completely ruined and Harmony would be awakened from her slumber. God knows that little girl needed to stay asleep as long as she could before they got to the event. If not, she was going to be cranky just like her daddy acts in the morning.

"I'm glad you finally came. I knew it was hard but it needed to be done. Now you can heal properly."

219

Kissing her hand once again, they drove in silence, both stuck in their own thoughts. Qy was thinking about tonight being the night that *Calvary Records* would be official. If it wasn't for God and the woman that he had beside him, there was no way that he would be able to live out his dream. When his first business was destroyed before it could even get off the ground good and then one thing after the next kept coming at him, causing more stumbling blocks in his journey for greater, it made him want to give in and he almost did. But God wasn't having it.

Come to find out, Anointed One, the producer he wanted to work with in the beginning, was Chey's cousin. She ended up reaching out to him about wanting him to meet her husband and when they got to the meeting, they were both floored. AO, or Nigel as Chey called him, was actually the son of her aunt who was murdered in the studio along with her mother. He was away visiting his father for the summer during the murders and they had lost touch. He was a few years older than Chey, but he never forgot her or her voice and they had reconnected recently. AO wanted Chey to be in the studio with him while he was producing his record. Once everything was completed, she had even recorded a track that she dedicated to her mother. Tonight would be the night that they would be debuting it. It amazed Qy just how God worked and it was definitely in mysterious ways.

Chey on the other hand was thinking about how tough it was to lay those flowers down on both of the headstones of Natalia and her baby boy. He didn't even have a chance at life, all because of the decisions his mother had made. Chey wondered if Natalia had taken the identity of her son's father to her grave with her. Qy was excluded along with both JJ and Jaxon so there was no telling who the man could be. But she wasn't mad anymore at Natalia. Chey realized holding on to the problems that her once best friend was dealing with were her own, and she couldn't take that burden for her even if she had wanted to.

It still hurt her that they didn't have time to make things right between them and deep down inside, Chey really did love Natalia. Natalia just didn't love herself. Mother Gladys and Cecil didn't want to turn the baby over, but he was getting too sick and they couldn't help him. They had prayed that it wasn't too late but it was. He passed not too long after Natalia was buried and they made sure to put them side by side. Maybe she could be a better mother in heaven. It did give Chey peace though, to know that her killer was behind bars, so maybe she could rest in peace.

JJ was doing three life sentences somewhere out of the state of Georgia. Being that he had killed both his mother and Natalia and attempted to take Jaxon's life, the judge threw the book at him. He didn't even want to go to trial and he just took his sentencing. Everyone knew that it was an open and shut case and obviously he wasn't too far gone to where he didn't know that his fate was already awaiting him. Maybe during his time in lockup, God could speak to him and change his heart—who knew.

Chey freed her mind of all of the things she was thinking because this night was about her husband, as she checked her face in the visor just before the cameras began to flash in their direction.

"You ready, baby?" she asked, smiling at her husband. She saw he was looking a little nervous and she understood. Leaning over, she blessed him with one of the most passionate kisses she could give while people were snapping pics through the windshield. She bet that would make The Shade Room before the night was over, if it wasn't already there.

"Come on," he smiled as he jumped out and grabbed his sleeping beauty from her seat. Harmony was the prettiest little girl he had ever seen. Her long thick hair was just like her mother's, but that was where the resemblance ended. She was all Qyree. She had his eyes, nose, smile, complexion and everything. He knew he should have named her Qyreesha because she was his little "mini me" but her name suited her. She definitely brought harmony to all of their lives.

"Here, give me my goddaughter so you can get these pics poppin', Mr. CEO," Tank said, taking his baby girl out of his arms.

"I mean you 'bout to be in these pics too, Mr. COO," Qy said, dapping him up. The dream that the two of them had since they were little boys was finally their reality, and they were doing it together.

"Oh, me and wifey already did our thing."

"What I tell you about calling me that? I am not your wifey boy, I'm your wife. I'm classy based like that," Von corrected him and swung her hair over her shoulder.

"You are glowing, sis," Chey said to Von. Indeed, she was glowing, but a happy marriage and a new baby on the

223

way did that to her.

At first she was so upset that she had gotten pregnant a year after they had gotten married. They tried so hard to prevent it because they didn't want their baby to suffer and be born with something they would have to live with for the rest of their lives. Tank always wanted a child of his own, but when he said that he was happy to have Amir, he really meant it. Even he was scared when they found out they were expecting.

They had used all of the birth control possible and by the time she had found out, it was too late to terminate although they were both sick thinking that would be an option. Once they found out that there would be ways they could try and prevent the baby from having the virus, they warmed up to the idea. They figured that God had his reasons and they would just trust His process. He hadn't led them astray so far and they knew that He never would. So in another month, they would be welcoming their daughter, Faith, into their lives, and Amir was ecstatic to be a big brother.

"Qy, hurry up, baby, we are about to start," Zaria said coming down the white carpet. To think that he almost lost her only a little while ago, no one would believe it looking at her now. Zaria was back to looking like her old self, only happier. Her hair was full again, her natural glow was back, and she had picked her weight back up in the right places.

Zaria was enjoying being a grandmother and couldn't wait until her other baby came. She made sure to tell Von and Tank that Faith would be her baby, too, just like she had Harmony and Amir. Amir even called her Mimi, 'cause she didn't like the word grandma. She said she was too fly for that and they couldn't help but to laugh.

"Man, y'all better come on before I get up on this stage. You know I haven't forgotten how to put on a show," Jaxon said.

Qy guessed it was true. God really did take care of babies and fools because he had taken care of Jaxon and let his mother tell it, he was the biggest fool ever. He almost didn't make it when JJ had shot him and he wouldn't have had the officer who shot JJ with the bean bag rounds waited a second later. It was because of that his shot was off, and the bullet that hit Jaxon missed his heart by less than a half of an inch.

When Chey was discharged from the hospital with their daughter and Zaria was back home as well, she made sure to tell them that they needed to go see him and make peace. Qy and his mother gave her hell for days about it, but she didn't back down until they went to see him. When they had gotten there, he was so close to the end of his rope, but their presence caused him to beg for their forgiveness. He had just told God that if He was real to show him, and not even ten seconds later, in walked his wife and son.

He apologized to them over and over again for hours, and even some days he still does. Jaxon finally realized that because he was not in his rightful place as the man of his home like God intended, everything in his life was exposed to the hands of the enemy. Because of him, he had subjected everyone that was connected to him to be attacked, and things would not line up until he did what God needed him to do.

Jaxon and Zaria may not have been married any longer, but they were the best of friends. They had vowed to be the parents that Qy needed and to be the best grandparents that their grandbabies deserved. He may not have gotten it right with his son, but he felt like God gave him another chance to do right by him by giving him a new life.

Standing in front of the closed double doors leading to

the room where so many people had come to celebrate this night with Qy and everyone he loved, he took a deep breath.

"Alright y'all, let's go save some souls with this music," Qy said as he walked into his purpose.

The End

From the Author

So y'all know I just cried at my own ending, right? I just want to thank everyone that continues to be on this journey with me. From book one all the way to this 14th one has been a fight, but I was able to draw strength from the love and support of my readers. I always say that if I can reach just one soul for God, then my work is done, but it's not. God requires more from me. I want to save as many as I can for the Kingdom before my time here on this earth is done, and I thank Him for giving me the means to do it with His help. I know that everyone won't receive what I write and that is ok, but for the ones that do, I pray that each word I write helps to change your life and bring you closer to God.

As always, thank you to my amazing husband Byron and our four beautiful children (Jalen, Elijah, Mekiyah, and Isaiah) for pushing me into greatness and being with me every step of the way. This is our success!

My Anointed Inspirations and Royalty family, thank you! When I feel like giving up, I can look to you all for encouragement. Through my mistakes, you still fight with me and we learn together. I don't always get it right and I will absolutely tell you when I mess up, but you all hold me down. I appreciate you and this success belongs to you all as well. The more doors that open for me I will gladly slide y'all right on in, too!

Most of all I thank God. It is because of Him that I am able to do what it is that I am doing. If I left it up to my own ability I would have stopped at book one but he wouldn't let me. The pushing, stretching, pulling, bumping, all of the stuff that doesn't feel good when He does it, I know is for my good and His glory. So I will continue to let Him have His way in my life.

Thank you to my readers!! Y'all are so demanding, I swear...lol! But I couldn't do it without you guys. Thank you for all of the support that you give me on the regular by purchasing each book I put out. LeBron may have won the MVP awards last night, but y'all the real MVPs!

May the blessings of God continue to overtake you all the days of your lives!

Love,

Dee

Heaven Between Her Thighs
Denora Boone

Looking for a publishing home?

Royalty Publishing House, Where the Royals reside, is accepting submissions for writers in the urban fiction genre. If you're interested, submit the first 3-4 chapter

s with your synopsis to submissions@royaltypublishinghouse.com.

Check out our website for more information:

www.royaltypublishinghouse.com.

Heaven Between Her Thighs
Denora Boone

Heaven Between Her Thighs
Denora Boone

CPSIA information can be obtained
at www.ICGtesting.com
Printed in the USA
LVOW05s2139110117
520606LV00013B/356/P

9 781539 833796